“What Are You Up To? Why Are You Here, In My Bedroom?

“Why are you telling everyone in town that we’re married?”

“*Your* bedroom,” she muttered, inhaling so sharply her towel opened wide and swished silently down her body.

Hunter got one more good look at full, high breasts. His own body sat up and howled. Then she muttered a curse, grabbed the towel and wrapped herself up again.

“Your bedroom? That’s a good one. I’ve been living in this suite of rooms for a year now, and funny, but I don’t remember seeing you.”

“A year? You’ve been pretending to be my wife, living in my house, for a year?”

What the hell was going on around here?

Dear Reader,

I'm so proud to be a part of Harlequin's 60th anniversary celebration! As a member of the Silhouette family, I'm delighted to be able to write romances with interesting characters, memorable stories and especially, happy endings.

For sixty years, Harlequin books have provided an escape from the everyday world. They've shown us that true love exists. That fidelity is still important. That promises made should always be kept. The Silhouette Desire line provides drama, comedy, passionate love stories and, most importantly, hope. Hope that no matter what else is going on in the world, love continues to be the goal all of us strive for.

In *An Officer and a Millionaire,* you'll meet Hunter Cabot, Navy SEAL. Hunter's a loner and he likes it that way. His only family is a grandfather he rarely sees. Until he gets a sixty-day leave, goes home and discovers that he also has a wife he's never met.

Margie Donohue is a loner, too—the only difference is that she's tired of being alone. She's looking for a place to belong. When her "husband" shows up unexpectedly though, she may be forced to give up the home she's finally found.

I hope you enjoy Hunter and Margie's story—I had a lot of fun writing it! Please visit my Web site at www.maureenchild.com and let me know what you think of the book!

And happy anniversary, Harlequin!

Maureen Child

MAUREEN CHILD

AN OFFICER AND A MILLIONAIRE

Published by Silhouette Books
America's Publisher of Contemporary Romance

Recycling programs for this product may not exist in your area.

ISBN-13: 978-0-373-76915-5
ISBN-10: 0-373-76915-6

AN OFFICER AND A MILLIONAIRE

This edition published by arrangement with Harlequin Books S.A.

Visit Silhouette Books at www.eHarlequin.com

Printed in U.S.A.

Books by Maureen Child

Silhouette Desire

†*Scorned by the Boss* #1816
†*Seduced by the Rich Man* #1820
†*Captured by the Billionaire* #1826
††*Bargaining for King's Baby* #1857
††*Marrying for King's Millions* #1862
††*Falling for King's Fortune* #1868
High-Society Secret Pregnancy #1879
Baby Bonanza #1893
An Officer and a Millionaire #1915

Silhouette Nocturne

‡*Eternally* #4
‡*Nevermore* #10

†Reasons for Revenge
††Kings of California
‡The Guardians

MAUREEN CHILD

is a California native who loves to travel. Every chance they get, she and her husband are taking off on another research trip. An author of more than sixty books, Maureen loves a happy ending and still swears that she has the best job in the world. She lives in Southern California with her husband, two children and a golden retriever with delusions of grandeur.

To Silhouette Desire Readers,
You've made all of this possible with your loyalty
and your enthusiasm for what we do!
Thank you all.

One

Hunter Cabot, Navy SEAL, had a healing bullet wound in his side, thirty days' leave and apparently a *wife* he'd never met.

On the drive into his hometown of Springville, California, he stopped for gas at Charlie Evans's service station. That's where the trouble started.

"Hunter! Man, it's good to see you! Margie didn't tell us you were coming home."

"Margie?" Hunter leaned back against the front fender of his black pickup truck and winced as his side gave a small twinge of pain. Silently then, he watched as the man he'd known since high school filled his tank.

Charlie grinned, shook his head and pumped gas. "Guess your wife was lookin' for a little 'alone' time with you, huh?"

"My—" Hunter couldn't even say the word. *Wife?* He didn't have a wife. "Look, Charlie…"

"Don't blame her, of course," his friend said with a wink as he finished up and put the gas cap back on. "You being gone all the time with the SEALs must be hard on the ol' love life."

He'd never had any complaints, Hunter thought, frowning at the man still talking a mile a minute. "What're you—"

"Bet Margie's anxious to see you. She told us all about that honeymoon trip you two took to Bali." Charlie's dark brown eyebrows lifted and wiggled.

"Charlie…"

"Hey, it's okay, you don't have to say a thing, man."

What the hell could he say? Hunter shook his head, paid for his gas and, as he left, told himself Charlie was just losing it. Maybe the guy'd been smelling gas fumes for too long.

But as it turned out, it wasn't just Charlie. Stopped at a red light on Main Street, Hunter glanced out his window to smile at Mrs. Harker, his second-grade teacher, who was now at least a hundred years old. In the middle of the crosswalk, the old woman stopped and shouted, "Hunter Cabot, you've got yourself a wonderful wife. I hope you appreciate her."

Scowling now, he only nodded at the old woman—the only teacher who'd ever scared the crap out of him. What the hell was going on here? Was everyone but him *nuts?*

His temper beginning to boil. He put up with a few more comments about his "wife" on the drive through town before finally pulling into the wide, circular drive leading to the Cabot mansion. Hunter didn't have a clue what was going on, but he planned to get to the bottom of it. Fast.

He grabbed his duffel bag, stalked into the house and paid no attention to the housekeeper, who ran at him, fluttering both hands. "Mister Hunter!"

"Sorry, Sophie," he called out over his shoulder as he took the stairs two at a time. "Need a shower; then we'll talk."

He marched down the long, carpeted hallway to the rooms that were always kept ready for him. In his suite, Hunter tossed the duffel down and stopped dead. The shower in his bathroom was running. His *wife?*

Anger and curiosity boiled in his gut, creating a churning mass that had him moving forward without even thinking about it.

He opened the bathroom door to a wall of steam and the sound of a woman singing—off-key. Margie, no doubt.

Well, if she was his wife…Hunter walked across the room, yanked the shower door open and stared in at a curvy, naked, temptingly wet woman.

She whirled around to face him, slapping her arms across her naked body while she gave a short, terrified scream.

Hunter smiled. "Hi, honey. I'm home."

"Who—what—how—who—"

"Now, honey," he drawled the words out, completely enjoying watching the shock ripple across her features, "is that any way to greet your husband?"

"I—I—"

He had her nervous—that was for damn sure, he

told himself. Easy enough to see by the way her eyes darted from one side of the room to the other, as if looking for an escape route.

Well, there wasn't one. She wasn't going anywhere until he had some answers. But that wasn't to say he couldn't make her as uncomfortable as possible. No better than she deserved for pretending to be his wife, for God's sake.

The shower area was directly behind her, and steam twisted in the air like fog. A quick glance around the once familiar bathroom allowed Hunter to notice the jars and bottles of lotions women seemed to be unable to live without. Plus, the black towels he preferred had been replaced with navy-blue. Not to mention a vase full of flowers in the corner of the marble vanity counter.

Looked as though she'd made herself damned comfortable in his home, too. Which meant she'd been lying to his grandfather. Damn it. Fresh anger churned in his gut, and he had to fight to contain it. This naked, curvy, all-too-delectable woman had been lying to a lonely old man. Probably wormed her way into his affections and was no doubt stealing him blind to boot. Well, her game, whatever it was, was up. He didn't care how good she looked naked. Well, he cared, but not enough to let himself get sidetracked.

He took a step closer and caught the delicious scent of her. Jasmine, if he wasn't mistaken, and something inside him stirred. It had been a while since he'd had a woman. He'd been too busy with mission after mission and hadn't wanted to bother. But now, with a naked, wet, terrific-smelling woman within arm's reach, his body was snapping to attention despite the fact that he was as furious as he was aroused.

She was watching him as though she were a rabbit and he a cobra.

So, she was perceptive as well as a liar.

"What, no kiss?" he asked, moving in even closer. If she dropped one arm, he'd have another look at her high, full breasts. "Didn't you miss me, honey?"

She jerked a quick look behind her, saw no help there and whipped her head back around to glare at him. The action sent tiny droplets of water flinging from the ends of her dark red, curly hair, and they hit Hunter's face like raindrops.

"You just keep your distance, you...*pervert*."

"Pervert?" He snorted a laugh and wiped the water from his face with one hand. "I'm just a husband trying to greet his *wife*."

"There's no greeting going on here. At all." Sidestepping fast, she snatched a navy-blue towel off the closest rod and wrapped it around herself in the blink of an eye.

Too bad. Hunter had enjoyed the view and the glimpse of peaked pink nipples he'd had just before she'd covered up. If nothing else, his "wife" had a body designed to make a man want to spend some time exploring those curves.

Now, though, she was managing to look down on him even though she was a full foot shorter than he was. The ice in her emerald-green eyes was enough to give a lesser man frostbite. But Hunter had the fires of righteous anger on his side, so he wasn't moved. Meeting her stare with an icy glare of his own, he demanded shortly, "Who the hell are you?"

"Who am I?" She whipped her head to one side, and her soaking wet hair swung back and out of her eyes, spraying Hunter with another spill of droplets. Frantically, she tucked one end of the towel into the valley between her breasts. But she was breathing so hard, the terry cloth shield she was obviously depending on didn't look any too stable. "I'm in *my* bathroom taking a shower, minding my own business when— Oh, God." Her eyes widened. "You're…I can't believe I didn't recognize you right away. But you scared me and—"

He flicked another lazy glance at her now scantily clad body. "Babe, if I scared you, you had it coming. Imagine how it felt for me to find out from every-damn-body in town that I have a *wife.*"

"Oh, for heaven's sake…"

"That about covers it," Hunter snapped, taking another step toward her. His voice was deceptively quiet. "See, I've got a month's leave coming. Decided to head home, do some recuperating, check in with my grandfather…" He walked a small, tight circle around her and enjoyed the watchful look in her eyes as she slowly turned in place to follow his progress.

"Imagine my surprise when everywhere I go in town, people are telling me how excited my wife is gonna be to see me."

"Well, I'm not. Excited," she added, as if he'd missed that. "More like irritated," she said. "Annoyed, really."

"Now that's a damn shame." Hunter stopped directly in front of her and did his best to loom. Wasn't difficult. Since he was taller than his "wife," forcing her to tilt her head back to look up at him was all too easy. "You think *you're* annoyed?"

"Wouldn't you be, when a perfect stranger sneaks into your shower like a scene out of the movie *Psycho*? All that was missing was that hideous, screechy violin music."

If she had been scared, she'd recovered now, Hunter thought. "I'm not the one in the wrong here, babe. You're the liar. You're the intruder."

"Is that right?" She sniffed, plopped both hands on her towel-covered hips and started tapping one bare foot against the bathroom rug.

"Straight up, that's right. You know damn well we're not married, so why don't you tell me what your scam is? And how the hell did you convince my grandfather to let you into the house?" The more he thought about it, the angrier he became. "Simon's nobody's fool, so you must be the queen of con artists."

"Con artist?" She slapped both hands against his chest and shoved. He didn't even sway in place. But her towel slipped a notch. He had hopes of another good look at her.

"If you think you're scoring points by acting all outraged," Hunter told her, his gaze dropping briefly to the slippage of her towel, "you're wrong."

She fumed silently for a second or two, and Hunter could have sworn he actually saw the wheels in her brain turning, calculating, figuring.

"You're not supposed to be here," she muttered.

"Oh, that's a good one, babe. I'm the one who's not supposed to be here?"

"You didn't tell Simon you were coming." She scowled at him. "And stop calling me 'babe.'"

"I'll call you whatever I damn well please. And you're lucky I'm not calling the cops."

Her mouth dropped open.

"As for my not letting Simon know I was coming, I consider that a good thing," he told her, meeting those hard green eyes with a cold look that should have frozen her on the spot. "Hard to catch a liar and a cheat if she knows you're coming."

"I am not a—you're really a very irritating man, did you know that?" She cocked her head to one side, and her wet hair hung in a curtain behind her. "No one in town ever mentioned that part of your personality. But then," she added, "you're scarcely here, so they've probably forgotten."

"I'm here now," he pointed out, ignoring the slight twinge of something uncomfortable. No, he didn't get back to Springville very often. He spent most of his time on base or being shipped out for various highly secret operations. Was he supposed to take a rare weekend off and drive all the way upstate only to turn around and drive back down again? He didn't think so. Besides, how he lived his life was none of this woman's business.

"This isn't about me, *babe.*" He used the word deliberately and enjoyed watching her cringe at it. "Let's get to the real questions. What the hell are you up to? Why are you here? In *my* suite? Why are you telling everyone in town that we're married, and how the hell did you fool my grandfather into believing you?"

"Your suite," she muttered, inhaling so sharply she loosened the towel enough that it opened wide and swished silently down her body.

Hunter got one more good, long look at full, high breasts, perky pink nipples and soft brown curls at the apex of her thighs. His own body sat up and howled. Then she muttered a curse, grabbed the towel and wrapped herself up again.

"Your suite? That's a good one. I've been living in this suite for a year now, and, funny," she added with a touch of sarcasm, "but I don't remember seeing you."

Screw her snide tone. He was concentrating on the words. "A *year?* You've been pretending to be my wife, living in my house for a year?"

Had it really been that long since he'd been home? Damn, guess it had been. But he'd talked to Simon every couple of weeks over the last year, and the old man had never once mentioned the woman masquerading as Hunter's wife. Not one syllable. Not a noun. Nothing. What the hell was going on around here?

Had she done something to his grandfather? Threatened him in some way? Hard to believe. Simon Cabot was as tough as three old boots. But he was older now. Maybe…

Hunter moved in even closer, riding a tide of fury that had the edges of his vision blurring. He looked down at her and had to admire the fact that she didn't back up. She didn't cower, even though she was far smaller than he, not to mention naked and all kinds of vulnerable. Her eyes flashed at him as if daring him to try to hurt her. It was almost like watching a toy poodle transform into a pitbull.

But admiration aside, he had to know what she was up to. "Play time's over, honey. Whatever scam you've been running, you're done. And if I find out you've stolen so much as twenty bucks from my grandfather, your cute little ass is going to wind up behind bars."

Steam was slowly sifting out of the room, and the air was chill enough to bring goose bumps to her still-damp skin. If she was feeling the cold, though, she ignored it. Lifting her chin, she said, "I'm not going to continue this conversation naked."

"Well, you're not leaving this room till I get some answers."

"I should have known you were a bully."

"Excuse me?" He actually *felt* his glower darken.

"Is this a military thing? You barking orders and expecting us poor civilians to jump into line? Well, I don't take orders from you. And you should be ashamed of yourself."

"Ashamed of myself? You might want to back off, *babe,*" he said, and it came out as more of a growl, "I'm not the one pretending to be something I'm not. I'm not the one living in someone else's home under false pretenses. I'm not the one—"

"Oh for heaven's sake, I'm not going to stand here and be insulted." She pushed past Hunter, giving him a straight-armed shove that caught him so off guard he actually stepped aside. He could have stood his ground, but then, he'd never been the kind of man to use his muscle against women.

His quick movement brought a twinge of discomfort from the still-healing wound in his side, and he automatically lifted one hand to it. Then he watched her storm out of the bathroom, somehow managing to look regal while wrapped in a towel. She left damp footprints on the thick, soft green carpet, which muffled the sound of her passage, and headed directly to *his* chest of drawers.

Wryly, he asked, "Going to be wearing some of my old boxers and T-shirts, are you?"

She shot him a surly look over her shoulder. "I moved your ratty old clothes to the bottom drawer a long time ago."

"Ratty?"

"What would you call T-shirts with more holes than fabric?"

"Mine."

She ignored him now, digging into an open drawer. Pulling out a pale blue lacy bra and a pair of panties to match, she hurried over to the huge walk-in closet, stepped inside it and closed the door behind her.

So he wasn't going to be watching her dress. Not that he wanted to. Fine. That was a lie. He wouldn't have minded another look at her figure. After all, he was human, wasn't he? And *male,* with an appreciation for a nicely rounded woman. And whoever the hell she was, he already knew she had some great curves.

Instantly, his mind filled with that last glimpse he'd had of her. Pale flesh, rigid pink nipples and a bottom that made a man want to grab hold and squeeze.

Scowling at the thoughts crowding his fevered mind, he shut them down resolutely. A Navy SEAL was nothing if not disciplined.

"Why are you here, anyway?" Her voice came from the depths of the closet.

"This is my home, babe. I belong here."

She snorted. That came through loud and clear. He also heard clothes hangers rattling and a hard thud followed by her muffled yelp.

"What're you doing?" he demanded.

"Breaking my toe," she snapped.

Hunter glowered at the closed door; then while he half listened to the sounds she made, he let his gaze slide around the room he'd grown up in. He'd been so distracted by the whole "wife" thing earlier that he hadn't really noticed how different the room was.

The walls were green, not beige. The carpet was green, not brown. There was a lacy quilt covering the king-sized bed he'd picked out himself at seventeen and a mountain of frilly pillows stacked against the headboard. Filmy white curtains fluttered at the windows that overlooked the garden at the rear of the mansion, and the French doors leading to the balcony boasted the same girly curtains as the windows.

How had he not noticed? He, whose very survival often depended on his observational skills? "What the hell have you done to this place?"

She stepped out of the closet then, and he whipped around to look at her. She wore a yellow T-shirt over a pair of worn, faded jeans that hugged every luscious inch of her and a pair of sandals that added about three inches to her measly height. Her green eyes were narrowed, her full mouth grim, and she'd somehow managed to fluff her wild mane of curly hair into a damp jumble of softness. When she folded her arms across her chest, his gaze locked on the wide, gold band on her ring finger.

Damn it.

Margie stared right back at him while she tried to ignore the rush of something hot and tempting inside her. His blue eyes were filled with suspicion he didn't bother to hide, and tension practically rippled off him in waves. Hunter Cabot was a lot...*bigger* than she'd expected. Not just tall. Big. His shoulders were wide, his chest and arms looked as though he spent most of his time lifting weights and even his long legs were thick and muscled beneath the black jeans he wore.

Impressive. And a little—no, a lot—daunting. But she wasn't about to let him know how nervous he made her. After all, she hadn't done anything wrong.

"Well?" He glared at her again. He really was very good at that. "Who the hell told you that you could move into *my* room and turn it into some female lair?"

The best defense, Margie had always believed, was a good offense. A lawyer she'd once worked for had taught her that, and she'd always found it to work.

"Your grandfather did," she answered with plenty of heat of her own. "You remember, the lonely old man you never visit?"

"Don't you start on me about my grandfather. You don't have the right."

"Really?" She marched right up to him, every step fueled by the anger she'd harbored for Hunter ever since she first came to work for his grandfather. "Well, let me tell you something, Captain Hunter Cabot, I earned the right to defend your grandfather the night he had his heart attack and *I* was the only one at his bedside."

He flushed. Anger? Or shame?

"Why were *you* at his bedside, anyway?"

Margie huffed out an impatient breath. She shouldn't be having to explain any of this. Simon had promised her that he would talk to Hunter before he came home. But this surprise arrival had thrown everything off.

"I'm Simon's executive assistant."

"His secretary?"

"Assistant," she corrected. "I was here. With him, when he had the heart attack. We tried to find you, but, big surprise, you were nowhere to be found."

"Just a damn minute..."

"No," she countered, stabbing her index finger at him, "you had your say; now it's my turn. You're never here. You hardly call. Your grandfather *misses* you, blast it. Why, I can't imagine—"

"That's none of your—"

"Not finished," she snapped, interrupting his interruption. "You're so busy running around saving the world you don't have time to be with your grandfather when he might have *died?* Like I said before. You should be ashamed of yourself."

Two

There, Margie told herself as Hunter's mouth snapped shut and his blue eyes flashed. He might have had the upper hand since the moment he'd found her naked—oh, dear God—in the bathroom. But now, it was as it should be: him having to defend himself.

The room was so suddenly quiet that she could hear them both breathing. Sunlight streamed in through the open French doors and lay in a golden slash across the spring-green carpet. A slight breeze ruffled the curtains and carried with it the scents of roses and columbine from the garden just below her bedroom. Normally, she loved this room, found it peaceful, relaxing. Today, not so much.

"I've got nothing to be ashamed of," he said tightly. "I'm off doing my job, serving my country. I'm not the one here taking advantage of a lonely old man."

"You don't know what you're talking about." Her voice was stiff and so was her spine.

"I don't know," he mused. "Seems pretty clear to me. You were his secretary and somehow convinced him that we got married. How you did it I don't have any idea, but I'm going to find out."

"Oh, that makes sense," she said. "I just threw a ring on my finger, said, 'Guess what, I'm married to your idiot grandson,' and Simon believed me. Tell me, do you think your grandfather is really that foolish? You must, which means you're not letting logic get in your way at all."

"Logic?"

"Never mind, it's probably something you're unfamiliar with."

A long minute ticked silently past as they stared at each other, but Margie was determined not to be the one to speak first. Her patience finally paid off.

His mouth worked and his features tightened until he looked as uncomfortable as any man could be before he said grudgingly, "About Simon's heart attack. I suppose I should…thank you, for being with him that night."

"You think?"

"I was on a mission," he added as if she hadn't spoken, "I didn't find out about his heart attack until I returned. Then the crisis was over. I called him, if you'll remember."

"Very touching," she snapped, remembering the pleased look on Simon's face when his grandson had finally called to check on him. "A deeply personal phone call. Yet, you still didn't bother to come and see him."

"He was fine," Hunter argued. "Besides, my team shipped out again almost immediately and—"

"Oh, I'm not the one who needs to hear your explanation," she told him, "It's Simon you should be talking to. Besides, I didn't stay with Simon during his illness for *your* sake."

"Fine."

"Fine." It felt…odd, to be standing in the same room with the man she'd been legally married to for a year. Hunter Cabot had for so long lived in her mind only that having him here in person was more like a dream than the reality she'd been living with.

Strange, but in all the times she'd imagined her first meeting with Hunter Cabot, she'd never once thought they'd be embroiled in a huge argument right off the bat. But he'd started it, calling her a thief! So she didn't regret any of the things she'd said to him. His features were still tight, but there was something else in his eyes besides anger now. Something she couldn't quite read, and that was a little unsettling.

"Where is my grandfather now?"

"Probably in his study," she muttered. "He spends most afternoons there."

He nodded and left without another word to her.

Margie's breath whooshed out in a rush as soon as he was gone and she hurriedly walked to the bed to plop down on the edge of the mattress. Staring down at her hands, she looked first at the wedding ring she'd picked out herself, then noticed her hands were shaking. Not surprising, really. Not every day she had a huge, gorgeous, furious man walk in on her in the shower.

"Naked. He saw me *naked*." That really wasn't the

way she'd wanted to meet her husband for the first time. Especially because she still hadn't found a way to lose those ten pounds she didn't need, and her hair looked hideous, and she didn't have any makeup on and—she groaned and slapped one hand over her eyes.

"For pity's sake, Margie, it's not like makeup would have transformed you into supermodel territory anyway." She knew exactly what she looked like. Her mouth was too wide, her nose was too small and the freckles spattered across her cheeks defied all known foundations. She was not the kind of woman a man like Hunter Cabot would ever notice. "But then, it doesn't matter what you look like, now, does it? It's not as though you're really married to the man." Legally, yes. Really, no.

She flopped back onto the bed and stared up at the cool green ceiling. She hadn't planned to meet her husband for the first time until *after* his grandfather had explained the whole situation. And it would've worked out just like it was supposed to have done if Hunter hadn't shown up two weeks early, for pity's sake.

So if you thought about it, this was all his fault.

But as Margie blindly stared at the ceiling, she had to admit that that knowledge didn't make her feel any better.

Hunter moved through the familiar halls with a long, determined step, but no matter how fast he walked, he couldn't leave that woman behind him. Her voice kept time with the hard thumps of his boot heels against the floor.

Lonely old man. Almost died. Ashamed.

Muttering curses under his breath, Hunter silenced that voice and hit the bottom of the stairs. Slapping one hand to the newel post, he made a sharp right turn and continued down the carpeted hall toward the last door on the left.

He opened the door without knocking and stepped inside. This room at least remained the same. Unchanged. Dark paneling on the walls, polished to a high gloss, gleamed in the sunlight pouring through the windows. Dark brown leather armchairs and sofas were sprinkled throughout the room, and behind the wide, mahogany desk where his grandfather sat, floor-to-ceiling bookcases displayed everything from the classics to fictional thrillers.

But Hunter's gaze locked on the smiling old man slowly pushing himself to his feet. "Grandfather."

"Hunter, boy! Good to see you! You're early," he added, coming around the edge of the desk with careful steps. "Didn't expect you for a couple of weeks yet."

Hunter walked to meet the man who had always been the one constant in his life. When he was twelve years old, Hunter's parents died in a car accident and he'd come to live with his paternal grandfather. Simon had stepped into the void in his grandson's life and had always seemed to Hunter to be larger than life. Strong, sure, confident.

Now, though, Hunter noticed for the first time that the years were finally catching up with his grandfather. Something cold and hard fisted around Hunter's heart as he hugged the older man and actually felt a new frailty about Simon. He swallowed back the questions crowding his throat and demanding release, and he forced himself to be patient.

Stepping back, the old man waved one hand at a chair and said, “Sit, sit. Are you sure you should be walking around with that wound in your side?”

“I’m fine, Grandfather,” Hunter said, reassuring Simon as he took a seat in the chair opposite him. He could wait for answers about the woman upstairs. For a moment or two, anyway. “Wasn’t more than a scratch, really.”

“They don’t put you in the hospital for four days with a scratch, boy.”

True, but he didn’t want Simon worrying anymore than he could help. Hunter had caught a bullet on his last mission, but it had been more painful than life-threatening. Now all that remained was an ache if he moved too fast and a scar from the hastily maneuvered field surgery he’d had to perform on himself, since he’d gotten separated from his team members.

Smiling, he said only, “They don’t let you out of the hospital after only four days if it’s serious.”

“That’s good, then. You had me worried, boy.”

“I know. Sorry.”

Simon waved the apology aside. “Nothing to be sorry for, Hunter. It’s your job, I know that.”

He still wasn’t happy about Hunter’s decision to join the military, though. Simon had wanted him to take over the Cabot family dynasty. To sit behind a desk and oversee the many different threads of the empire Simon’s father had started so long ago. But Hunter had never been interested in banking or any other kind of business that would tie him to a nine-to-five lifestyle. He’d wanted adventure. He’d wanted to do something *important.* Serving his country filled that need.

"Still," Simon was saying, with a touch of an all-too-familiar scheming note to his voice, "you're not going to be able to do this job forever, are you?"

Hunter scowled to see a calculating gleam in his grandfather's eyes. He hated to admit even to himself that he'd been thinking along the same lines lately. Frankly, since he was shot. Five years ago, it wouldn't have happened and he knew it. He'd have been quicker. Spotted the ambush sooner. Been able to get to cover fast enough to avoid the damn bullet that had nailed him.

But his career choices were not what he wanted to talk about. And since he couldn't think of an easy introduction into the subject at hand, he simply blurted out, "Forget my job for the moment. Grandfather, that woman upstairs is *not* my wife."

Simon crossed his legs, folded his hands together atop his flat abdomen and gave his grandson a smile. "Yes, she is."

"Okay, clearly this is going to be tougher than I thought," Hunter murmured and stood up. Rubbing one hand across the back of his neck, he reminded himself that the woman had had a year to worm her way into Simon's affections. It was going to take more than a minute to make him see the truth. "I've never *met* that woman, Grandfather. Whatever she's told you is a lie."

Simon smiled and followed Hunter's progress as he paced back and forth. "She hasn't told me anything, Hunter."

He stopped and shot his grandfather a hard look. "So you just let anybody who claims to be my wife move in and take over my suite?"

Simon chuckled. Probably not a good sign.

"You don't understand," the old man said. "She didn't lie to me about being married to you, because she didn't have to. I'm the one who arranged the marriage."

"You did what?" Hunter stared at his grandfather in complete disbelief. He didn't even know what to say. What the hell *could* he say? "You arranged—you can't do that."

"Can and did," Simon assured him, looking altogether pleased with himself. "The idea came to me after that heart attack last year."

"What *idea?*" Hunter walked back to his chair and sat down, his gaze pinned on the older man grinning at him.

Simon's white eyebrows lifted. "Why, the answer to my problem, of course. There I was, in the hospital. There you were, off only God knew where, and there was Margie."

"Margie."

"My assistant."

"Your—right. She told me that." Assistant turned granddaughter-in-law, apparently.

"Very organized soul, Margie," Simon mused thoughtfully. "Always on top of things. Knows how to get things done."

"I'll bet."

Simon frowned at him. "None of this was Margie's doing, boy. This was my idea. You remember that."

Hunter took a tight grip on his rising temper and forced himself to speak slowly and calmly. It wasn't easy. "What exactly was your idea?"

"I needed family here!" Shifting in his chair, Simon lifted one arm to the chair arm, and his fingers began to tap on the soft leather. "Blast it, decisions had to be made, and though I'd told Margie what I wanted, she didn't have the authority to make the doctors do a damn thing. Could have been bad for me, but I was lucky."

Instantly, Hunter's mind filled with images of Simon lying in a hospital bed, hooked up to machines that monitored his heart, his breathing, while doctors bustled and a short, curvy redhead tried to issue orders. He hated like hell that he hadn't been there for the old man when he'd needed Hunter most. But feeling guilt didn't mean he understood how he'd ended up with a wife!

"So, you could have given her power of attorney," Hunter said.

"Might have," his grandfather allowed, and his tapping fingers slowed a bit. "But I didn't. Instead, I convinced Margie to marry you."

"You—"

"It was the easiest way I could see. I want family around me, boy, and you're not here."

More guilt came slamming down on Hunter until he was half surprised he could breathe under the weight of it. Still… "You just can't marry me off without even mentioning it."

"I've got two words for you, Hunter," his grandfather said, "*—proxy marriage.*"

"Proxy? How can you even do that without my signature?"

"I got your signature," Simon told him with a sly smile. "And if you'd bother to read the Cabot financial papers I send to you for your signature, you'd have noticed the proxy marriage certificate."

Damn it. Simon had him there. Whenever the packets of papers arrived for him, Hunter merely signed where indicated and sent them back. The family business wasn't his life. The Navy, was. And he kept his two worlds completely separate. No doubt his slippery grandfather had realized that and exploited it. Admiration warred with irritation.

"Ah, good. You realize I'm right." Simon's fingers quickened, and the tapping on the old leather came fast and furious, belying the old man's attempt at a casual pose. "I stood in for you in the marriage ceremony. I knew that since you couldn't get home for my heart attack, you wouldn't have been able to get home for your own wedding—"

"—not that I was *invited…*"

"—my friend Judge Harris did the deed, and we kept it quiet. I sent Margie off on a week's vacation once I got better, and we put out that you and she eloped."

"Eloped."

"Worked out fine. Figured there was no rush in telling you."

"Especially since I didn't *want* a wedding."

Simon frowned at him and Hunter remembered being thirteen years old and standing in this very study, trying to explain why he'd hit a baseball through the study window. The same sense of shame and discomfort he'd felt then washed over him now. The only difference was he was no longer a kid to be put in his place.

"How'd she talk you into this, Simon?"

In answer, his grandfather pushed himself out of the chair, drew himself up to his full height and gave Hunter a look that used to chill him to his bones. "You think I'm some old fool taken in by a pretty face and a gold-digging nature? You seriously believe I'm that far gone, boy?"

"What else am I supposed to believe?" Hunter stood up too and met Simon's hard stare with one of his own. "I come home for a visit—"

"After two years," Simon threw in.

"—and you tell me you arranged to marry me off to someone I've never met just so you can have family close by?"

"You can watch your tone with me, boy. I'm not senile yet, you know."

"I didn't say you were."

"You were thinking it." Simon turned, walked to his desk and sat down behind his personal power center. From that very chair, Simon had run the Cabot family fortunes for more than five decades. "And I'll tell you something else. Margie didn't want any part of this. It was all my idea."

"And she went along out of the goodness of her heart." Sarcasm was so thick in Hunter's tone that even he heard it.

"'Course not. This was business, pure and simple. I'm paying her five million dollars."

"Five—" Hunter sucked in a gulp of air. "So she *is* in it for the money. And you said she's *not* a gold digger?"

"She damn well isn't, and you'll figure that out for yourself after you spend some time with her." Simon picked up a pen from the desk and twirled it absent-mindedly between his fingers. "Had to browbeat her into taking the money and doing this for me. She's a good girl and she works hard. She's done a lot of good for this town, too, and she's done real well by your name."

"How nice for me." Hunter shook his head at the sensation of a velvet-lined trap snapping shut around him.

"You should be grateful. I picked you out a wife who's a hard worker, and she's got a big heart as well."

"Grateful." Hunter moved in, leaned both hands on his grandfather's desk and ground out tightly, "What I'll be grateful for is a damn annulment, Simon. Or even a divorce. As soon as possible."

Disgusted, his grandfather muttered, "I should have known you wouldn't appreciate this."

"Yeah, you should've."

"If you'd open your eyes and see her as I do, you'd change your tune." Simon looked so damn smug, so self-satisfied that Hunter felt a surge of temper rise up and grab the base of his throat. For his whole damn life, Simon had been the one he could count on. The man who had taught him what *duty* and *honor* meant. The one who'd instilled in Hunter a sense of right and wrong. Now, he was blithely explaining how he'd set Hunter up with a marriage he didn't want all for Simon's own convenience.

"My 'tune' doesn't need changing," Hunter told him. "Just why the hell should I 'appreciate' having a wife I didn't want in the first place? One you're *paying*."

"I told you. She didn't want the money. Had to talk her into accepting it."

"Oh, yeah. I'll bet she was really hard to convince, too. Five million dollars? Damn it, Simon, what were you thinking?"

"You weren't here," the older man said softly. "I'm getting on, Hunter, and you weren't here. Margie is."

Again, he felt that soft, swift stab of guilt—then he buried it. "She's your secretary."

"She's more than that."

"Sure, *now,*" Hunter allowed.

"You don't know her," Simon said, and his voice was whisper soft. "She came here to build a life for herself and she's done it. And she's been a good wife to you—"

"I haven't been here!"

"—and a good granddaughter to me."

All right, he could at least admit that much to himself, Hunter thought. Gold digger or not, the curvy redhead had at least apparently been good to Simon. When Hunter had finally heard about his grandfather's brush with death, guilt had gnawed him for not being there when the old man had needed him. But the nature of his job meant that he couldn't always be around. He lived and died according to orders.

So, knowing that Simon hadn't been alone during that frightening time in his life was good. And for that, he could be grateful. Not that he'd be telling that to the curvy redhead with the quick temper.

"Margie deserves your respect," Simon warned, lifting one finger to point at him.

"For marrying a man she never met to keep her boss happy." Hunter nodded sagely. "Yeah, that spells respect to me."

Simon scowled at him. "You never did know enough to listen to me."

"I listen. I'm just not interested in what you're

saying. I don't want a wife." All right, he'd been doing some thinking about his future lately. Maybe he'd even considered getting married, for about thirty seconds. But thinking about doing something and actually doing it were two wildly different things. And if he did eventually decide to get married, he'd be the one picking out his own damn wife, thanks.

"You could do worse," Simon grumbled.

"Yeah? I don't know about that. A woman who has to be *paid* to marry me pretty much sounds like the bottom of the barrel."

"Shows how much you know about anything," Simon said, and his fingers tapped restlessly again. "Margie's the cream of the crop."

"Not much of a harvest around here, then," Hunter murmured, then louder, added, "I won't stay married to her."

Simon blew out a breath. "No, I didn't suppose you would. Though you should know Margie feels the same way you do."

Hunter wasn't so sure. She may have had the old man fooled but not him. With five million dollars at stake, a woman might be willing to do just about anything.

"She's been good to me, and I won't have you embarrassing her."

"Oh yeah. Wouldn't want to embarrass anybody."

His grandfather sighed dramatically, then kept talking as if Hunter hadn't said a word. "She's planned a big party for my eightieth birthday, and I don't want anything spoiling that, either."

"A hell of a lot of demands flying around here," Hunter said under his breath.

"So, until the party's over, I expect you to act like the husband everyone in town knows you are."

"Excuse me?" He hadn't expected that.

"You heard me. People in Springville like Margie. They respect her. And I'm not going to stand by and watch you make her a laughingstock. You'll be leaving again, no doubt—" He paused as if waiting for confirmation.

Hunter nodded. "I have to report back in about a month."

Another frown. "Well, I'll still be here and so will Margie, hopefully, so I don't want her life ruined because you were angry."

Hunter's back teeth ground together. "No, wouldn't want Margie inconvenienced."

Simon went on again, ignoring Hunter's comments completely. "If after the party you still want the annulment—"

"—I will."

"—I won't stop you and I'm sure Margie won't. But until then, you'll do this my way."

Hunter looked at his grandfather and recognized the *set-in-stone* expression on the old man's face. There wouldn't be any budging him on this one. Once Simon Cabot made up his mind about something, nothing less than a nuclear strike would change it. Irritation swamped Hunter, and the uncomfortable sensation of being trapped came right along in its wake.

But Simon was an old man. And Hunter owed him. So he'd do this his grandfather's way. He'd be here for the party, and then before he went back to the base, he'd set annulment proceedings into action.

"Fine." Hunter tamped down the frustration bubbling

within and swallowed back the urge to argue. "When I'm in town, I'll act married."

"You'll act it here, too."

"What?"

"You hard of hearing all of a sudden? You should get that checked." A sly smile curved Simon's mouth briefly before he became all business again. "As long as you're home, you're a married man. I won't have the servants treating Margie badly. Everyone in this household knows you're married."

Hunter was still reeling from that piece of news when a soft knock on the study door sounded out. He turned around as the door opened, and there stood his "wife."

Three

"Simon?" Margie asked, blatantly ignoring Hunter. "Is everything all right?"

"Fine, fine. I was just explaining the situation to Hunter."

"Good." Though judging from the look on the younger man's face at the moment, Margie thought he hadn't been too happy with his grandfather's explanation. Well, neither was she.

She hadn't wanted to marry Hunter, but she'd done it for Simon. And whether Hunter believed it or not, the five million dollars hadn't swayed her. What had convinced her to go along with Simon's plan had been the lost, *frightened* look in the old man's eyes that had convinced her to take part in what she'd recognized right away as a crazy plan.

And for the last year, she'd finally felt the sense of belonging she'd always wanted. She'd had a grandfather. A home. A place to call her own. People to care for—people who cared for her.

To Margie, that was priceless.

But she had to admit that being married to a Hunter who wasn't around was far easier than being married to the man in person. Looking at him now, he seemed too...big. His shoulders, his broad chest, his piercing blue eyes.

His scowl.

Frowning right back at him, she then shifted her gaze to Simon and said simply, "The doctor's here."

"Blast it." The older Cabot quickly picked up a sheaf of papers from atop his desk and busily started leafing through them. "Margie, tell him I'm too busy to see him today. Try me next week. Better yet, next month."

She smiled, since she was more than accustomed to Simon's frantic attempts to avoid his doctor. "There's no getting out of it, Simon."

"Is there a problem?" Hunter asked.

Margie reluctantly looked at him again, met his gaze and felt a bolt of something hot and wicked slice through her. The man had incredible eyes. Which, of course, meant nothing to her. Especially since great eyes did not make up for a crabby, arrogant nature. Still, he looked a little worried for his grandfather, and that was enough to touch Margie, so she hurried to reassure him. "No, it's just his checkup. The doctor comes here to see Simon every couple of weeks since Simon can't be trusted to keep an appointment in town."

"I'm a busy man. Too busy to go see a damn pill pusher," Simon muttered.

Hunter folded his arms over his impressive chest and asked, "Simon's all right, though? Healthy?"

Margie nodded and told herself not to look at that wide chest or the muscles so clearly defined beneath the soft fabric of his black T-shirt. "Yes, he's, uh..." She swallowed hard, cleared her throat nervously, then continued. "He's recovered completely. The checkups are just routine now."

"Routine," Simon muttered again. "What's *routine* about disrupting a man's life every time he turns around—that's what I want to know..."

"Good," Hunter said. "I'm glad everything's all right, but I'll want to talk to the doctor myself, of course."

"Why should *you* talk to him," Simon questioned. "He's *my* doctor and I don't need another babysitter," he added with a glare at Margie.

"Of course you will," Margie told Hunter as they both ignored the grumbling older man. Weren't they being polite all of a sudden, she thought. But she wasn't fooled. There was still something dark and smoldering in Hunter's eyes.

"Who's in charge here, I want to know?" Simon demanded.

"That would be me," a new voice announced.

Margie tore her gaze from Hunter's to see Dr. Harris striding into the room with a wide smile on his creased face. His wild gray hair was forever sticking up in odd tufts all over his head, and his soft brown eyes looked magnified behind his glasses. He walked straight up to

Hunter and shook his hand. "Good to see you back home, Hunter. It's been too long."

"Yeah," Hunter said, sliding a quick look at Margie, "it has."

"Wasted your time coming out here," Simon said, still shuffling papers. "Too busy for you today and don't need any more pills, thanks."

"Pay no attention to him, doctor," Margie said smiling.

"I never do." The doctor released Hunter's hand, then pulled Margie in for a quick hug. "Don't know what we would have done without your wife around here the last year or so, Hunter."

She stiffened as Hunter's gaze locked on her.

"Is that so?" he asked quietly.

"It is," Simon put in.

"The woman's a wonder," Dr. Harris said. "Not only sees that your stubborn old goat of a grandfather does what he's supposed to, but she also single-handedly helped us raise enough money to add an outpatient surgery annex to the clinic. Of course, she told us all how much *you* had to do with it."

"Did she?" One dark eyebrow lifted as he studied her, and Margie fought to keep from fidgeting under that stare.

"She did." Beaming now, the doctor added, "She let us all know that after Simon's heart attack, you wanted to be sure the clinic had everything it needed so locals didn't have to go into the city to be taken care of. Meant a lot to folks around here that you still think of Springville as your home."

"Glad I could help," Hunter said, tearing his gaze from Margie's to look at the doctor.

"Simon always said how you'd start taking more of an interest in the town one day," the man said with a clap on Hunter's shoulder. "Seems he was right. So I just want to thank you personally—and not just for the clinic but for everything else you've done—"

"Everything else?" Hunter asked.

"Dr. Harris—" Margie spoke up quickly to cut the doctor off before he could say too much. "Didn't you have other appointments today?"

"True, true," the man was saying, still grinning his appreciation. "So I'd better get down to business. Just wanted you to know the whole town appreciates what you're doing, Hunter. It's made a difference. All of it."

"*All* of it?" Hunter's hard, cold gaze locked on Margie. "How much is *all?*"

"Aren't you here to plague me?" Simon snapped. "Or are you going to stand there and talk to Hunter all day?"

The doctor chuckled. "He's right. Why don't you two go off somewhere together while I examine this crotchety patient of mine?" He winked at Hunter. "Lord knows if I had a pretty little wife I hadn't seen in months, I'd want some alone time with her."

"Just what I was thinking," Hunter said, and Margie inhaled sharply.

She really didn't want any more alone time with Hunter at the moment. In fact, she was good. She could have waited days, or maybe forever, to be alone with him again. Unfortunately, it didn't seem as though she'd be getting that wish granted.

"Come on, *honey,*" he said, taking her elbow in a hard grip, "let's go get 'reacquainted.'"

She only had time to throw one quick look over her

shoulder at Simon before Hunter started propelling her across the room. Simon gave her a thumbs-up signal and a Cheshire cat grin—not much as life preservers went but better than nothing.

Hunter's legs were so long that she had to practically run to keep up with him, but Margie managed, barely. They slipped out of the study, and Hunter reached behind her to close the doors before he looked at her again.

Hard to believe, but there was both fire and ice in his eyes when he said, "You've got some explaining to do, babe."

"I told you not to call me that." If he thought she was going to simply curl up in a ball and whimper for mercy, he was sadly mistaken. He'd taken her by surprise when he'd shown up in the bathroom earlier, so she'd babbled too much. But she'd had time now to think. To gather her own sense of outrage along with her self-confidence. She hadn't done anything wrong. But Hunter Cabot couldn't say the same.

She took a quick look around the empty hallway, hardly noting the lavish furnishings that had, the first time she'd stepped into the castlelike Cabot home, completely intimidated her. How far she'd come, she thought idly, that she now felt at home here, with the rose-patterned Oriental rugs dotted on a gleaming wood floor. With the pale washes of color seeping through the stained-glass windows in the foyer. With the crystal vases holding arrangements of flowers that were nearly as tall as she was.

This castle had become her home, and she refused to let Hunter take that feeling away from her.

"I don't owe you anything," she said, keeping her tone calm and dispassionate, which wasn't easy.

His mouth curved in a smile that had nothing to do with humor. "Now see, that's not the right tack to take."

"How about this one, then? You're hurting me," she said, with a glance down to where his fingers were clenched around her elbow. Instantly, Hunter's grip on her elbow loosened. Not that he actually let her go, but the strength in his fingers eased up a bit.

"Sorry." He blew out a breath and glanced all around the empty hallway before dipping his head to speak to her again. "But after everything Simon just told me, I think you and I need to talk."

"Simon explained everything?" Thank heaven. He was supposed to have had this chat with Hunter *before* the man came home, and that would have made this situation a lot easier. But if Simon had told his grandson what was going on, what was left to talk about?

"Yeah, but that doesn't mean I'm cool with it, so like I said, start talking."

Now that he wasn't holding her so tightly, it was easy enough to pull herself free of his grasp. So she did, then took a step backward for good measure. "I don't know why I should explain myself to you when Simon's already done it."

"I can think of a reason. In fact," Hunter added, "I can think of *five million* reasons."

She blanched. "You don't seriously believe I'm doing this for the money?"

"Why wouldn't I?"

Margie sucked in a breath. "Why, you self-righteous, judgmental, arrogant son of a—"

His narrowed gaze flicked past her briefly; then he grabbed her, yanked her close and kissed Margie so hard she almost forgot to breathe.

Sensation raced through her bloodstream until every inch of her body was standing up and shouting *Yippee!* Her stomach dropped, her heartbeat thundered in her chest and her mind fuzzed out so totally, she couldn't have given her own name if asked.

Her whole world had come down to the feeling of Hunter's mouth on hers. His tongue pushing past her lips to sweep inside her warmth. His breath sliding into her. His arms wrapped around her like taut wire, binding her to his body, until all she could do was lift her own arms to hook them behind his neck.

She opened to him eagerly, hungrily, reacting solely to the passion he'd ignited. Didn't seem to matter that he was insulting, annoying and a bully. All that counted now was what he was making her feel. Never before had she reacted so completely to something so simple as a kiss. But then, this was no simple kiss, either.

There was heat and fire and lust and fury all rolled into one incredible ball of energy that felt as though it was consuming her.

Then it was over as quickly as it had begun. She staggered a little when he let her go. Not surprising, really, since he'd kissed her blind. "What? How? What?"

His lips quirked at one corner of his mouth before he again looked past her and said, "Sophie!"

Oh, God. The housekeeper, Margie thought, instantly feeling a flush of embarrassment.

But Hunter dropped one arm around her shoulders

and pulled her in close to his side as he greeted the older woman. "I was so busy getting reacquainted with my *wife,*" he was saying. "I didn't see you come up."

How was he able to joke and laugh and speak coherently after what they'd just experienced? Margie looked up at him and couldn't believe that he was so unmoved by what had happened. How could he not have felt what she had? How could something that powerful be so one-sided?

"Oh, don't you worry about that," Sophie said. "It's good to see two such lovebirds canoodling."

Canoodling?

"I'm so glad to have you home again. Now you two go on upstairs, and we'll see you for dinner, all right? Cook's making all of your favorites, Mr. Hunter." Sophie gave him a quick hug. "We're all so happy to have you home again. Aren't we, Margie?"

Hunter finally looked down at her, and Margie saw the light of challenge in his eyes. "That right, babe? Are you happy to have me home?"

Margie still felt shaky from that kiss, but she didn't want to let him know how he'd affected her. Especially since that kiss had seemed to mean nothing to him. So she met his look with one of her own, then forced a smile she didn't feel. "Oh, *happy* doesn't even begin to describe what I'm feeling."

Dinner took forever.

Simon was at the head of the table acting like Father Christmas or something, and Hunter's "wife" was sitting directly opposite him, alternately ignoring him and sending him looks designed to set his hair on fire.

As for Hunter, all he could think was, he never should have kissed her.

Damn it.

Ever since tasting her, the only thing he wanted was another taste. And that couldn't happen. No way was he going to hook himself even deeper into this little fiasco his grandfather had arranged. For all he knew, his little "wife" was counting on seducing Hunter into making this a real marriage. Maybe that was her grand plan.

But how could it be her plan when it had been *his* idea to kiss her? Gritting his teeth, he avoided looking at the woman across from him and tried to draw his mind away from the memory of her mouth on his. Useless. He'd been trying for hours to forget exactly how he'd felt when his mouth had come down on hers. To brush aside the near electrical jolt of pure, white hot lust and desire that had threatened to crush him.

Hell, if it hadn't been for Sophie standing there in the hall, he might have pushed Margie up against a wall and...

Way to not think about it, he chided himself.

His body was hard and achy, and his mind was still spinning from the effect she'd had on him. She'd fit into the circle of his arms as though she'd been made for him. The taste of her lingered in his mouth, and the memory of the feel of her curves pressed along his body had kept him hard as stone for hours.

She wasn't at all the kind of woman he usually went for. So Hunter couldn't explain even to himself why he was suddenly so filled with the need to touch her again. To kiss her again. He should be thinking about strangling her for what she was doing here in this house.

Instead…

Damn it. Even as he looked across the table at her, wearing a shapeless blue dress with a high collar and short puffy sleeves, his mind was stripping away her clothes. Laying her bare on the fussy quilt that now covered his bed. In his mind, he was kissing every curvy inch of her, burying himself inside her and—

And, if he didn't turn his thoughts to other things, he'd never be able to stand up from this table without showing the world just how much he wanted her.

Grimly, Hunter fought for control. He looked at her again and tried to see past the softly curling dark red hair and bright green eyes. He shoved aside the memory of how she'd felt in his arms and instead tried to figure out how much of her "I'm innocent" act was for real. On the surface, she seemed to be exactly what she was portraying. A young woman doing a favor for a lonely old man. But for all Hunter knew, she was just a hell of a good actress. And if she was playing him, how much easier it would have been for her to play Simon.

They never had gotten around to having their "talk" earlier. After kissing her, Hunter hadn't trusted himself to be alone with her. So instead, he'd taken one of the horses Simon still kept and went for a ride over the property. Not that the long ride had done a thing for his sanity. Because images of Margie had ridden with him every step of the way.

"More wine, Hunter?"

Hunter looked at his grandfather and nodded. "Yeah, thanks."

But he knew even as more of the dark red wine was poured into his glass that there wasn't enough liquor in the world to ease the wild, churning thoughts running through his brain. Why her? he asked himself. Why this short, argumentative con artist? Hell, he'd just finished a relationship with Gretchen, a six-foot-tall model with the face of an angel and even she'd never gotten to him as deeply as this one tiny redhead had.

Gritting his teeth, he took another bite of the pot roast prepared just for him. It might as well have been cardboard. He'd been looking forward to coming home. Having a few days to relax and not worry about a damn thing. Well, that was shot, he told himself. Everywhere he went in the damn house, someone was winking at him or smiling knowingly.

Having every servant in the house treating him like a newlywed was annoying. Having his "wife" within arm's reach and untouchable was irritating. Hell of a homecoming.

The last mission he'd been on, Hunter had been wounded, cut off from his team, and he had had to find his own way out of hostile territory. Eight days he'd been alone and fighting for his life—and what he was going through now made that time seem like a weekend at Disneyland.

"There's a dance at the end of the week," Simon said, dragging Hunter gratefully from his thoughts. "To celebrate the new addition to the clinic."

"That's nice." He didn't give a damn about a dance.

"Now that you're here, you'll take Margie to represent the family," Simon said.

"I'll what?" Hunter looked at his grandfather and out of the corner of his eye noted that Margie looked just as surprised as he felt.

"Escort your wife to the town dance. People will expect it. After all, you and Margie are the ones who made it all possible."

"I didn't have anything to do with it," Hunter reminded the older man.

Simon bristled, narrowed his eyes on him and said, "As far as people in town are convinced, you did."

"He doesn't have to go with me," Margie said quickly, apparently as eager as Hunter was to avoid any extra amount of togetherness. Now why did that bother him?

"I'll just tell everyone he hasn't recovered from his injuries," she added.

Now it was Hunter's turn to scowl. Not that he wanted to go to the damned dance, but he didn't want someone else, especially *her,* making up excuses for him. The day he needed help—which would be never—he'd ask for it.

"Damn good at lying, aren't you?" he asked.

She turned her head to spear him with a long look. Then giving him a mocking smile, she admitted, "Actually, since I've had to come up with dozens of reasons why you never bother to come home to see your grandfather, yes, I have gotten good at lying. Thank you so much for noticing."

"No one asked you to—"

"Who would if I hadn't?"

"There was no reason to lie," he countered, slamming his fork down onto the tabletop. "Everyone in town knows what my job is."

She set her fork down, too. Calmly. Quietly. Which only angered him more.

"And everyone in town knows you could have gotten

compassionate leave—isn't that what they call it in the military?—to come home when Simon was so sick."

Guilt poked at him again. And he didn't appreciate it.

"I wasn't even in the country," he reminded her, grinding each word out through gritted teeth.

She only looked at him, but he knew exactly what she was thinking, because he'd been telling himself the same damn thing for hours. Yes, he'd been out of the country when Simon had his heart attack. But when he'd returned, he could have come home to check on the older man. He could have taken a week's leave before the next mission—but he'd settled instead for a phone call.

If Hunter had made the effort, he would have been here to talk his grandfather out of this ridiculous fake marriage scheme and he wouldn't now be in this mess.

With that realization ringing in his mind, he met Margie's gaze and noted the gleam of victory shining in those green eyes of hers.

"Fine. You win this one," he said, acknowledging that she'd taken that round. "I'll take you to the damned dance."

"I don't want—"

"Excellent," Simon crowed and reached for Hunter's wine glass.

"You can't have wine, Simon," Margie said with a sigh and the old man's hand halted in midreach.

"What's the point of living forever if you can't have a glass of wine with dinner like a civilized man?"

"Water is perfectly civilized." Apparently, Margie had already forgotten about her little war with Hunter and was focused now on the old man pouting in his chair.

"Dogs drink water," Simon reminded her.

"So do you."

"Now."

"Simon," Margie's voice took on a patient tone and was enough to tell Hunter she'd been through all this many times before. "You know what Dr. Harris said. No wine and no cigars."

"Damn doctors always ruining a man's life for his own good. And you," he accused, giving Margie a dirty look, "you're supposed to be on my side."

"I am on your side, Simon. I want you to live forever."

"Without having any damn fun at all, I suppose," he groused.

Hunter watched the back-and-forth and felt the oddest sense of envy. His grandfather and Margie had obviously had this same discussion many times. The two of them were a unit. A team. And their closeness was hard to ignore.

He was the odd man out here. He was the one who didn't belong. In the house where he'd grown up. With his grandfather. This woman…his "wife," had neatly carved Hunter out of the equation entirely.

Or, had he done that himself?

It had been a hellish day, and all Hunter wanted at the moment was a little peace and quiet. Interrupting the two people completely ignoring him, he said, "You know what? I'm beat. Think I'll head up to bed."

"That's a good idea," Simon agreed, shifting his attention to his grandson. "Why don't both of you go on up to your room? Get some rest?"

Silence.

Several seconds ticked past before one of them managed to finally speak.

"*Our* room?" Margie whispered.

Hunter glared at his grandfather.

Simon smiled.

Four

"I'm not sleeping on the floor," Hunter told Margie.

"Well," Margie said from inside the closet, where she was changing into her nightgown, "you're not sleeping with *me*."

Good heavens, how could she possibly share a bed with the man who'd kissed her senseless only hours ago? If he kissed her again, she might just give into the fiery feelings he engendered in her and then where would she be?

"Don't flatter yourself, babe," he said, loud enough to carry through the heavy wooden door separating them. "It's not your body I'm after. It's the mattress. Damned if I'm sleeping on the floor in my own damn room."

She frowned at the closed door and the man beyond

it. Apparently, she didn't have anything to worry about. He had clearly not felt anything that she had during that kiss. Was she insulted? Or pleased? "Fine. I'll sleep on the floor."

"Help yourself," he countered.

Margie stopped in the process of tugging her nightgown over her head. "You'd let me, wouldn't you? You'd let me sleep on the floor rather than do it yourself like a gentleman."

"Never said I was a gentleman," he told her.

"Well, I'm not sleeping on the floor." This was her room now. Had been for over a year. Why should she be the one to be uncomfortable? And if he wasn't interested in her sexually, she should be perfectly safe. Right?

"Up to you."

"Just don't you try anything," she warned, telling herself to pay attention.

He actually laughed. "Trust me when I say you're safe."

Bastard. How easily he dismissed her. That kiss he'd given her clearly hadn't touched him at all. Even though her own lips were still humming with remnants of sensation. Of course it hadn't meant anything to him. Why would it? She'd known most of her life that she simply wasn't the kind of woman men like him noticed.

She was too short, too…round. He probably went for the six-foot-tall, ninety-pound type who thought a single M&M was a party. His kind of woman never had the last cookie in the box; she didn't *buy* cookies. His kind of woman didn't wear T-shirts; she wore silk. And her clothes hung on her as if she were a coat hanger. No bulges, no curves, no lines. His kind of woman didn't have to marry a man by proxy; she had men lining up at her door. And his kind of woman wouldn't have melted at a simple kiss.

"Oh God, how did I get myself into this?"

Being married to Hunter when he wasn't there had been so easy. So perfect. She'd made him into the ideal husband. Thoughtful, caring, loving. How was she supposed to have known that the real man was light-years away from the image in her mind?

And yet, this Hunter stirred something inside her that made her yearn for things to be different. Which was just a one-way ticket to misery and she knew it. The only way she would ever have a husband like Hunter was this way. A lie.

Still grumbling to herself, she stepped out of the closet to find her "husband" already ensconced in the bed. On *her* side.

"Move over," she commanded, waving one hand for emphasis.

"It's a king-size bed," he reminded her. "Plenty of room for both of us."

Oh, she thought, there probably wouldn't be enough room for her to lie down comfortably beside him if the bed were the size of the *county.* But she wouldn't let him know that she was feeling decidedly uneasy about this situation. Besides, she was going to have enough trouble falling asleep tonight, let alone having to sleep on the wrong side of the bed.

"You're on my side."

He looked around, then shrugged broad, bare shoulders. "Since I'm the only one lying on it, I figure it's *my* side."

His eyes shone with amusement in the pale wash of light from the bedside lamp. His bare chest gleamed like old gold, and when he shifted higher onto the pillows, the quilt covering him dipped, pooling at his hips.

Margie sucked in a gulp of air but couldn't quite stop herself from admiring the view. The soft, dark hair on his chest narrowed into a strip that snaked across his abdomen, then disappeared beneath the quilt.

He was naked.

Oh, God. She was never going to get to sleep tonight. Her stomach did a slow roll and pitch, and her mouth went dry. "Don't you have pajamas?"

He chuckled and she couldn't help noticing the dimple in his left cheek. Why did he have to have a dimple?

"No," he said, "I don't." Then his gaze swept over her, taking in her knee-length, long-sleeved cotton gown decorated with pale blue flowers. His eyes widened as he lifted his gaze to meet hers. "Don't you have something less…"

Margie felt his disapproval plainly, plopped both hands on her hips and dared him to finish that sentence. "Less *what?*"

"Less…*Little House on the Prairie?*"

She smoothed one hand over her comfy nightgown. Didn't she feel pretty? He couldn't make it any clearer that he wasn't experiencing the slightest bit of attraction for her. "There's nothing wrong with what I'm wearing. It's very cute."

One dark eyebrow lifted. "If you say so."

"And comfortable."

"Okay."

Margie huffed out a breath, finished doing up the buttons on the front of her perfectly sweet nightgown, then glared at him again. No doubt he was used to going to bed with women who were either naked or wearing bits of lace and silk. "Are you going to move over or not?"

"Not."

"You are the most insensitive, arrogant—"

He deliberately closed his eyes and snuggled his head into *her* pillow. "We've been over this already. How about we just put off the insult exchange until morning?"

"Fine."

"Fine. Now get into bed and go to sleep."

Muttering darkly under her breath, Margie walked around the wide bed to the absolute wrong side. It didn't bother him at all to share the bed with her. He'd already closed his eyes to dismiss her. He couldn't have made it any clearer that he was in no way interested in her. So why was she shaking and nervous? This was so not fair.

He'd tossed all of her decorative throw pillows to the floor, and she had to kick them out of her way as she moved. Before she could get into bed, Hunter reached over and flung the quilt back for her, incidentally providing her with yet another look at his long, tanned form just barely hidden by the strategically placed quilt.

And when she was finished admiring his leanly muscled body, she finally noticed the stark white bandage affixed to his left side, just above the hip. Somehow, she'd managed to forget during their argument that he'd been wounded recently, and for some reason she felt bad for harassing him in his condition.

"Are you—do you—" She stopped, blew out a breath and looked into his eyes. "Is your wound all right? I mean, are *you* all right?"

"I'm touched by your concern," he said, clearly untouched. "Yes, I'm fine, though not quite up to sexcapades just yet. So like I said, you're safe." His gaze dropped over her nightgown again and he shook his head. "Though even if I wasn't laid up, I'd have to say that your choice of nightgown is the best male-repellant I've ever seen."

Instantly, Margie regretted worrying about him at all. He was insulting, rude and arrogant, and she hoped his side ached like an abscessed tooth. And if she ever again felt those stirrings inside her, she'd squash them like a bug. "You're—"

"Insults in the morning, remember?"

"Fine." She swallowed back everything she wanted to say to the completely irritating, totally sexy man in her bed and turned instead to pick up the pillows he'd so carelessly tossed to the floor.

"What're you doing now?"

She didn't even look at him, just continued picking up the pillows and stacking them in a line down the center of the bed. When they were all in place, she smiled at a job well done. "I'm building a wall between us," she said. "As you pointed out, it's a king-size bed. Plenty of room for us *and* a wall."

"You don't need a wall, babe; you've got the nightgown."

"Maybe you need it," she told him, sliding onto the sheets and drawing the quilt up to her chin.

"Yeah?" he asked as he turned out the light and plunged the room into darkness. "Afraid you'll ravish me in your sleep?"

She closed her eyes and turned onto her side, giving him her back. "Afraid I'll murder you. Sleep tight."

The next morning Margie was back in the closet getting dressed when Hunter stepped out of the shower. Rummaging through his duffle bag, he pulled out a worn, faded pair of jeans and a dark blue T-shirt with the words *Navy SEAL* emblazoned across the front.

"I have to go into town this morning, see to a few details about the dinner dance," Margie called out from what had become her own private dressing room.

"Let me guess," he said. "You're in charge of that, too."

From what he'd been able to tell, Margie "Cabot" had insinuated herself into everything she could. What was the plan, here? Why would she be bothering with getting involved with the doings in Springville if she was married to him only for the five million dollars Simon had promised her?

Shaking his head, he ruefully admitted that he had even more questions about her than he had the day before. Starting with, why was he so attracted to a woman he probably wouldn't have noticed under normal circumstances?

"Why is it so hard for you to understand that some people actually *like* being a part of the community?"

"I just don't get why *you* want to do it." He shot a

look at the partially opened door and tried not to think about what she was doing in there. But images of her wet, naked, lush body kept filling his head. Plus there was the memory of her kiss and the soft, open eagerness she'd met him with.

His body went stiff and hard as stone almost instantly and groaning, Hunter adjusted his jeans. It didn't help much. Damn it, what he needed was a woman, not a wife. It had been a long two months since he'd been with a woman, and right now it felt more like two years.

Hell, it was a good thing he woke up early every morning, because that wall she'd built between them had come tumbling down sometime during the night. Hunter'd been surprised to find that he'd instinctively turned to her in the darkness, pushing those pillows aside and wrapping himself around her. Thankfully, she'd still been sleeping when he woke up and had the presence of mind to rebuild that stupid wall.

"Why wouldn't I want to contribute where I can?" she demanded, stepping out of the closet to face him.

Hunter stared at her for a long minute. Morning sunlight slanted in through the lacy curtains on the windows and shone down on his wife in all her frumpy glory. She wore a shapeless box of a black suit, the hem of which hit her knees. The white blouse under her jacket was buttoned to her throat.

And even with all that, he felt a short zing of something hot and dangerous. How the hell was she able to do that to him? Even the gorgeous Gretchen hadn't elicited a response like this.

Irritated that his own body was betraying him at every damn turn, he snapped, "Are you secretly a nun?"

"What?" She looked confused.

Hunter started for her and did a slow walk around, taking in the ugly suit from every side. "First your nightgown. Now, this thing."

She folded her arms under her breasts, giving them definition enough that he had to pause to admire them. Instantly, a memory of hard, pink nipples caressed by drops of water filled his mind and tortured his body a lot farther south.

"There's nothing wrong with this suit," she argued.

Except for the fact that it was hiding an amazing body. But if he had any sense, he'd be grateful for that fact, not so resentful.

"Nothing that a good fire wouldn't cure."

She inhaled sharply and Hunter admired the view. His slow smile told her that too, so she dropped her arms to her sides, and instantly the shapelessness of her clothes hid her physical charms.

"Seriously," he said. "Why do you hide that body?"

"Excuse me?" A faint flush of color filled her cheeks, and despite everything, Hunter was charmed. He hadn't known women could blush anymore.

He tucked one finger under her chin and lifted her face to his. Those eyes of hers fascinated him even while he knew that he shouldn't get even more involved with her. Wasn't it enough, he thought, that he was married for a month? Wasn't it more than enough that he was hot and hard and achy for her? But why shouldn't she feel the same discomfort he was going through?

"You forget, babe. I've *seen* that body of yours. I know it's got curves and valleys and some great..." He grinned and finished, *"hills."*

She pulled away from his touch, and Hunter rubbed the tip of his finger as if he could still feel the cool silk of her skin on his. "So why are you hiding it?"

"I'm not hiding anything," she argued, walking across the room to the dressing table. She took a seat on the padded stool, picked up a wide-toothed comb and dragged it through her long curls. "I just don't draw attention to the fact that I need to lose ten pounds."

Women. None of them were ever happy with their bodies, he thought wryly. Even Gretchen was constantly on a diet, and remembering her now, he realized that she was so damn skinny it was a wonder he hadn't cut himself on her bones when he'd held her. Sex with Margie, on the other hand, would be a lush experience. All those curves. All that soft, smooth flesh to explore and enjoy.

He grimaced as his body went even harder and felt more uncomfortable than before. Shaking his head, Hunter walked up behind her and leaned down to plant his hands on the dressing table. He was so close behind her that his chin rested on top of her head as his gaze met hers in the mirror.

"Don't you know covering up only makes a man wonder what's under all that fabric?"

As her gaze locked with his, he watched her swallow hard before saying, "As you just reminded me, you already know what's hidden."

A slow smile curved one side of his mouth as he realized she was embarrassed. Would a liar and a thief be so easily discomforted? Interesting thought. "And that body deserves better."

"Thanks for your opinion," she said and slipped out from underneath him by ducking under one of his arms. Then she grabbed her purse and stationed herself by the door. "I've got to go, so I suppose I'll see you later."

"I'll go with you."

"What? Why?"

He wasn't entirely sure himself. All he knew was that he wasn't ready for her to leave just yet. She was watching him warily, and in that oversize suit, she looked…vulnerable, somehow. Hunter had the urge to somehow protect her. Which was completely unreasonable and he knew it. She didn't need protection, he reminded himself sternly. She needed getting rid of. Which he would do at the end of a month. For now, though, she was his wife whether he wanted one or not, and they both might as well get used to it.

"I was going to go into town myself today. See some old friends."

"Oh."

"But I've changed my mind," he told her as he studied the ugly black suit she wore. "I think we'll go into the city instead."

"San Francisco?"

"That's the one," he said and walked to the side of the bed. Sitting down, he pulled on one boot first, then the other, and stamped his feet into them. Standing up again, he looked down at her as she asked, "Why?"

"To get you some decent clothes."

"I don't need new clothes."

"Now see, we're arguing again," he pointed out. "You won last night's round, but I'll win this one."

"Hunter—" She stopped and frowned slightly as if saying his name had actually felt odd to her. "There's no reason to buy me new clothes. What I have is perfectly serviceable."

"That's where you're wrong." He walked up to her, tipped her chin up again and smiled down into green eyes that flashed with irritation and suspicion. "See, babe, you're my wife. And my wife doesn't dress frumpy."

She blinked at him. "Frumpy? This isn't frumpy. This is a business suit."

"If you say so." He took her arm, turned her toward the door and started walking. What the hell did he care what she looked like? His brain was shouting at him, but apparently he wasn't going to listen. He wanted to see her in clothes that fit her, that showcased not just her body but the woman inside, too.

And just who was that, he asked himself as he stared into her eyes. Liar? Cheat? Or was she simply what she claimed to be? A woman doing a kindness for an old man? Hunter already knew she was strong. She stood toe-to-toe with him and never gave an inch, and he had to admire that almost as much as he admired the way she could set his body on fire with merely a glance.

"I don't want to shop."

He stopped dead, gave her a quick grin and said, "That may be the first time I've ever heard a woman say those words."

"You're not going to charm me into this."

"You think I'm charming now? Last night you threatened to kill me in my sleep."

"I didn't say you were charming," she corrected primly. "I said you were trying to use charm. Badly."

"Ah, there's the wife I know and loathe." The words

were out before he could stop them. And the instant he said them, he wished he hadn't.

She pulled free of his grasp, and he winced at the fury in her eyes. "I know you don't like me, but you don't have to be mean."

Hunter studied her eyes and finally saw more than her anger. He saw hurt in those depths too and regretted causing it. He'd been so busy concentrating on his own feeling of entrapment, the constant state of arousal, which he blamed solely on her, he hadn't really considered that she was as locked into their "performance" as he was. At least for the time being.

And he had the nagging feeling that maybe she wasn't the liar and cheat he thought she was. Even a practiced con artist would have a hard time worming her way into Simon's heart, which she had obviously done. Not to mention what she'd pulled last night.

Building that wall of pillows between them hadn't been the act of an adept thief. She'd behaved more like a vestal virgin trying to protect her virtue from a marauding horde. So what the hell was really going on? Who was she, really?

What if he was wrong about her? Well, he told himself firmly, for one thing, he didn't *want* to be wrong about her. It would make this so much easier if she was just what he suspected she was. In it for the money. But then, even if the five million dollars was her sole motivation, she was now faced with living the lie she'd built.

Couldn't be comfortable for her, either.

So did he give her the benefit of the doubt? Or did he continue to make both of them miserable for a full month? Neither, he decided. He'd give her enough rope, then stand back to see if she actually hanged herself with it. He could be patient. Hell, his training, his job, his *life* usually demanded patience. So he'd back off on the verbal attacks and see how she reacted.

"You're right," he said at last and had the pleasure of seeing surprise flicker across her face. "I'm sorry."

She studied him for a long second or two, obviously trying to decide if he meant it or not. But finally, she nodded. "It's okay. It's a weird situation. For both of us."

"Just what I was thinking." Interesting. Be a little more accommodating, and she was far less prickly.

"So. Truce?" she asked.

"Maybe," he said thoughtfully. "I'll let you know when we're finished shopping."

"Hunter…"

He shook his head. He wasn't going to let go of this one. "My wife doesn't dress like that," he said, waving one arm to indicate the hideous suit she seemed so attached to. "I'm not going to have everyone in town wondering why in the hell I won't buy you new clothes. You want to play the part of Mrs. Cabot? You'll do it looking a hell of a lot better than this."

She lifted her chin and glared at him, but whatever she was going to say remained unuttered.

"Good choice," he said with a brief nod. "You're not going to win this one."

Margie felt Hunter's hand on the small of her back as clearly as if it were a live electrical wire. Spears of heat as wild and unpredictable as lightning bolts kept shooting through her system, and it was all she could do to walk and talk despite the distractions.

Main Street in Springville was waking up after a winter that had been cold and gray and bleak. Now in springtime, the sun shone out of a brilliantly blue sky, a cool wind danced down the street and bright bursts of flowers filled the planters at the feet of the street lamps. Colorful awnings stretched out over the sidewalk in front of the stores, and clusters of neighbors gathered together to chat.

She loved this town. Had from the moment she'd first arrived two years before. It was like a postcard of small-town American life. A flag waved in the center of town square, moms with strollers sat on benches, laughing at toddlers wobbling around on the grass, and the scent of fresh bread baking drifted through the bakery's open door.

After growing up in Los Angeles, just one more face in an anonymous crowd, coming to Springville was like finding an old friend. She belonged here. She fit in. Or at least, she told herself with a sidelong glance at the man beside her, she *used* to.

Now, she knew that she wouldn't be able to stay once this month with Hunter was up. She'd have to leave this town, these people, even Simon, the grandfather she'd come to love. Because staying after the divorce would be impossible. She wouldn't be able to stand the pitying looks from her friends. She wouldn't be able to answer the questions everyone would have.

And mostly, she wouldn't be able to stay in the place where all of her lovely fantasies had died.

"Still say we should have gone to the city," Hunter murmured, then waved at someone across the street.

Margie shook her head. She'd agreed, finally, to shopping, but had insisted that they do their buying in town. "You're a Cabot," she said for the third time. "You should support the local businesses."

"You make me sound like a king or something. What does being a Cabot have to do with where I shop?" His voice was low, but she had no trouble hearing him. In fact, Margie had the distinct feeling that she would always be able to concentrate easily on the deep rumble of his voice.

In just twenty-four hours, she'd already become attuned to him. Oh, God. What a mess.

She smiled and nodded at an older woman they passed on the sidewalk, then muttered, "Your family built this town. The headquarters of your business is here. You employ half the people who live here."

"Not me," he insisted, "Simon."

"The Cabots," she reminded him.

"Oh, for—"

"Hunter!"

"Now what?" he muttered, stopping and draping one arm around Margie's shoulder.

They'd already been stopped countless times by people excited to see Hunter back home. The heavy weight of his arm on her felt both comforting and like a set of shackles, binding her to his side. And how was that possible? How could she feel desire for the very man who was making her life a misery?

A young couple, James and Annie Drake, holding hands as they hurried up the sidewalk, grinned at Hunter and Margie as they approached. The man had brown hair and thick glasses, and his grin was reflected in his eyes. "Hi Margie. Hunter, it's good to see you back."

"Good to be back, James," he said, and the tone of his voice was almost convincing.

Except that Margie knew he didn't really want to be here. So who, she wondered, was acting now?

"Annie, good to see you, too. How're the kids?"

"Oh, they're fine," the tall blond woman said, smiling at Margie. "Just ask your wife. She helped me ride herd on them during the last council meeting."

"It was no trouble," Margie put in, remembering the three-year-old twins, who were like tiny tornadoes.

"Is that right?" Hunter asked.

"Don't know what this town did without her," Annie said. "She's helped everyone so much. And she has so many amazing ideas!"

Margie gave her friend a wan smile and wished Annie would be quiet. She could feel the tension in Hunter's arm, and it was getting tighter.

"Oh, now that I believe," Hunter said with a squeeze of her shoulders. "She's just full of surprises."

"Oh, yeah," James added, "Margie's a wonder."

"So I keep hearing."

Hunter's arm around her shoulders tightened further, and Margie deliberately leaned into him, making his gesture seem more romantic than he meant it to be. The fact that the moment she was pressed to his side, heat spiraled through her system like an out-of-control wildfire was just something she'd have to keep to herself.

"Well, we know you're busy," James was saying. "We just spotted you and wanted to thank you personally for everything you're doing for the town. Folks really appreciate it."

"Yeah," Hunter said thoughtfully. "About that…"

Was he going to admit to these nice people that he hadn't had a thing to do with making their lives better? Would he tell them that Margie had been making up his involvement?

Annie interrupted him. "Just having the new day care center at Cabot headquarters has been a godsend," she said, slapping one hand to the center of her chest as if taking an oath. "Margie told all of us how important you felt it was that the mothers who worked for you be able to leave their kids in a safe place. Somewhere close where the moms could work and still be close to their children."

"Did she?"

Margie felt Hunter's gaze on her but didn't turn her head up to look at him, afraid she'd see anger or disgust or impatience in those cool blue eyes of his.

Tears swamped Annie's eyes, but she blinked them away with a laugh. "God, look at me. Getting all teary over this! It just means a lot to all of us, Hunter. I mean, I need the job, but having the kids nearby makes working so much easier on me."

"Good," he murmured. "That's real good, Annie, but the thing is…"

"See, honey," Margie said quickly, determined to stop Hunter before he could disavow himself of everything these people were feeling. "I told you, everyone in town is so pleased that you're taking an active interest in Springville."

"She's right about that," James said. "Why, the newly redone Little League field and all of the flowers planted along Main Street…" He stopped and shook his head. "Well, it just means something to know that the Cabots are still attached to the town they built, that's all."

"Hunter's happy to do it," Margie told them, smiling and leaning even harder into her husband's side.

"We just wanted to thank you in person," James said, tugging his wife's hand. "Now, we've got to run. Annie's mom is watching our two little monsters, and she's probably ready to tear her hair out by now." Nodding, he said, "It really is good to see you, Hunter."

"Right. Thanks." Hunter stood stock-still on the sidewalk as the happy couple hurried off, and Margie felt the tension in him through the heavy arm he kept firmly around her shoulders.

"Well," Margie said softly, trying—and failing—to peel herself off Hunter, "I suppose we'd better go on to Carla's Dress Shop now."

"In a minute," Hunter said, tightening his arm around her until she could have sworn she could feel every one of his ribs, every ounce of muscle, every drop of heat pouring from his body into hers. "First, I want you to answer something for me."

She swallowed hard, tipped her face up to his and found herself caught in his gaze. "What?"

"Why'd you do it?" he asked, features stony, eyes giving away nothing of what he was feeling. "Why'd you let everyone think that it was my idea to do all these things around town? Why didn't you just do whatever it was you do without dragging me into it?"

"Because I'm your wife, Hunter," she said. "It only

made sense that you be a part of all of the decision making."

"But I never asked for this," he argued, his eyes going icy as he looked at her. "I didn't—don't—want to be responsible for this town."

Margie shook her head and saw more than she guessed he would want her to. Whether he would admit it or not, he loved this place, too. She'd seen it in his face as they walked along the familiar street. She'd heard it in his voice when he greeted old friends. And she'd felt it from him as the Drakes offered their thanks for everything *he'd* done for them and everyone else.

"Don't you see, Hunter," she said softly and reached up to cup his cheek, voluntarily touching him for the first time. "It's not about what you want. It's about what they need. The people in Springville need to feel that they're important to the Cabots. And like it or not, you *are* the Cabots."

Five

"Nonsense," Simon said. "There's no reason for you to leave, and I won't accept your resignation."

Margie sighed. She'd known that telling Simon she'd be leaving at the end of the month wouldn't be easy. But after spending several hours in Springville with Hunter, she'd realized that she'd never be able to stay once her "marriage" was over. How could she?

Once Hunter left, every time she went into town, she'd have to see pity on the faces of her friends. They'd talk about her and speculate about what had gone wrong in her "wonderful" marriage.

She just couldn't stand the thought of it. This place had been a refuge for her. A place where she'd found friends and a sense of belonging she'd never known before. She didn't want any of that to change. So to protect herself and her memories of this place, she had no choice but to leave.

"You have to accept it, Simon." Margie shook her head sadly. "I'll be leaving at the end of the month. I have to."

"No, you don't," the old man said, lips pinched as if he'd bitten into a lemon. "Hunter's not an idiot, you know. He'll open his eyes. See you for who you are. Everything's going to work out fine. You'll see."

If a part of her wished he were right, she wouldn't admit to it. Because her rational mind just couldn't believe it. She and Hunter hadn't exactly gotten off to a smooth start. "Simon, he thinks I'm a gold digger."

The old man barked out one short laugh. "He'll get past that fast enough. I told him I had to force the money on you."

"About that," she said, wincing inwardly. Margie had never wanted the five million dollars, but Simon had been adamant about her accepting it. All she'd ever wanted was an honest job and to be able to support herself.

She hadn't married Hunter for the money. She'd done it for Simon. And, she admitted silently, because she'd liked the idea of being married. Of being wanted.

Stupid, Margie, really stupid.

She should have known that she had been walking into a huge mistake.

"Don't you worry about my grandson, you hear me?" Simon said, pushing up from the chair behind his desk. He walked slowly toward her, linked his arm through hers and headed toward the door. "I've known Hunter all his life, and I'm sure he's going to do the right thing."

"According to him, the right thing is to have me arrested."

He laughed again and patted her arm. "Just trust me, Margie," he told her, ushering her into the hallway. "Everything's going to work out."

"Simon—"

"Not another word, now," he admonished, holding up one hand to still anything else she might have to say. "You just be yourself and let me worry about Hunter."

Then he closed the study door, shutting Margie out and leaving her to wonder if he'd even heard a word she'd said. Probably not. She'd learned in the two years she'd worked for Simon that his head could be every bit as thick and stubborn as his grandson's seemed to be.

For the next few days, Hunter suffered through oceans of gratitude. Stoically, silently, he accepted the thanks from people he'd known his whole life for things he hadn't done.

Margie had been right, he knew. The people in Springville did need to know that their jobs, their lives, were safe. And around here, that meant having the Cabot family take an interest. Be involved.

And his "wife" was the Queen of Involved. She was on a half dozen committees, spent some of her day with Simon, taking care of business matters, and then what time she had left, she devoted to being the Lady of the Manor.

Hell. Hunter rubbed one hand across his face and told himself to knock it off. Yes, he resented all of the time and effort she was putting into Springville, but this was mainly because he still hadn't figured out why she was doing it. And why was she giving him so much credit for everything she'd done? What the hell did she care if people in town hated or loved him? What did it matter to her if the Little League field had been replanted and new dugouts constructed for the kids who would play there this summer?

Why was she so damn determined to carve a place for herself in this little town? And why was she dragging him along with her?

It's not about what you want, Hunter. It's about what they need.

Those words of Margie's kept repeating in his mind, and he didn't much care for it. He'd never thought about the town and his attachment to it in those terms, and a part of him was ashamed to admit it, even to himself.

"But damn it, I don't need a teacher. Don't need this woman who's not even my wife making me look good to a town I don't even live in anymore." He shook his head, glared out at the wide sweep of flowers spread out in front of him and muttered, "I didn't ask her to do it, did I? I didn't ask to be the damn town hero."

"You talking to yourself again, Hunter?"

His head snapped up, and his gaze locked on the estate gardener watching Hunter from behind a low bank of hydrangeas. How much had the man heard? How much did he know? This pretending to be something he wasn't was driving him nuts. Just as being married to a curvy, luscious redhead he couldn't touch was beginning to push him to the edge of his control.

Sleeping beside her every night, waking up every morning to find himself holding her close only to jump out of bed and rebuild her damn wall before she could wake up and discover his weakness.

Weakness.

Since when did he have a damn weakness?

Taking a breath, he told himself to play the game he'd agreed to play. To get through the rest of the month and reclaim his life. When the month was over, he'd find a woman. Any woman, and bury his memories of Margie in some anonymous sex. Then he could get back to the base and do what he knew best.

"Just what planet are you on, Hunter?"

The gardener's voice came again and Hunter muttered a curse he hoped the older man couldn't hear. "Didn't see you there, Calvin."

Not surprising, since the man was practically hidden behind the massive pink and blue blooms dotting the rich, dark green leaves of the bushes.

"Don't see much of anything since you've been home, if you ask me," Calvin said, dipping his head to wield his pruning shears. The delicate snip of the twin blades beat a counterpoint to the lazy drone of bees dancing through the garden.

Hunter shoved both hands into the pockets of his jeans and walked toward the old man who'd been in charge of the Cabot gardens for nearly forty years. "What's that supposed to mean?"

"Hmm?" Calvin lifted his head briefly, shot him a glance and shrugged. "Just seems to me a man who's been apart from his wife for months on end would spend more time with her and less wandering around the estate talking to himself, that's all."

Hunter sighed. "That's all?"

Calvin's bristling gray hair wafted in the cool breeze, and his pale blue eyes narrowed on Hunter. "Well no, now that I think on it, maybe that's not all."

Hunter reached out, ran one finger along the pale pink petals of the closest blossom and slid a glance to the old man watching him. "Let's have it, then."

"You think I don't notice things? I'm old, boy, not blind."

"Notice what, Calvin?"

"How you watch that little girl of yours when she's not looking. How when she *is* looking, your eyes go cold and you look away."

Hunter scowled. Since when had Calvin become so damn perceptive? "You're imagining things."

"Now I'm senile, then? Is that what you're trying to say?"

"No," Hunter said quickly, then shoved his hand back into his pocket. Tough to be a hard ass with a man who'd known you since you were a kid. "It's just...complicated."

Calvin snorted a laugh. "You always did make bigger mountains out of mountains, boy."

"What?" Hunter laughed shortly as he tried to figure out what Calvin was talking about.

"No molehills for you. Nope. You look at something hard and make it impossible. Never could see what was right in front of you for staring out at the horizon. Always looking for something even though you wouldn't know it if you stumbled on it."

Hunter would have argued, but how could he? The old man was too damn insightful. Hunter had spent most of his life looking past the boundaries of this estate to the world beyond Springville. He'd wanted...more. He'd wanted to see other places, be someone else. Someone besides the latest member of the Cabot family dynasty.

And he'd done everything he'd wanted to, hadn't he? He'd done important things with his life. He'd made a difference. Shifting his gaze across the garden and the wide stretch of neatly trimmed grass that ran down to the cliff's edge and the sea beyond, he thought how small this place had once seemed to him. How confining. Strange that at the moment, it looked more welcoming than anything else. As if this place had simply lain here, waiting for him to come home.

Hunter frowned thoughtfully and wondered just why that notion all of a sudden felt comforting.

"Calvin?"

The sound of Margie's voice shattered Hunter's thoughts completely. He turned toward her and felt something inside him shift, like a bolt pushing free of a lock.

She stood in a slice of sunlight on the stone patio and Hunter's breath caught in his throat. She wore a green silk shirt with an open collar and short sleeves, tucked into a pair of form-fitting linen slacks. Her incredible hair was lifting in the wind caressing her, and it danced around her head like a curly, auburn halo. Her grass-green eyes were fixed on him as he stared at her and Hunter couldn't stamp out the hunger she was probably reading on his face.

Why the hell had he bought her new clothes?

Margie's heartbeat thundered in her chest, and her mouth went dry under Hunter's steady stare. Even from a distance, she saw him clench his square jaw as if fighting an inner battle for control. And somewhere inside her, she preened a little, knowing that just looking at her was in some small way torturing him.

At first she'd been uncomfortable wearing clothes that defined her too-voluptuous—in her opinion—figure. As if she were walking around naked or something. She wasn't used to people—*men*—looking at her the way Hunter was now. Always before, she'd sort of blended into the crowd. She'd never stood out, never been the kind of woman to get noticed.

For the first time in her life, Margie actually felt pretty. It was a powerful sensation. And a little frightening. Especially since Hunter didn't look too happy with whatever he was thinking.

Well, she reminded herself, it was his own fault. He was the one who'd insisted on buying out half of Carla's Dress Shop. He was the one who'd approved or vetoed everything she'd tried on. Which had really annoyed her until she'd gotten into the spirit of the thing and had pleased herself by watching his eyes darken and flash with hunger every time she appeared in a new outfit.

The arrogant, bossy man had, it seemed, painted himself into a corner of his own design.

"Did you need something, Margie?"

"What?" The voice seemed to come from nowhere. Hunter's gaze was still locked on her, and he hadn't spoken—she was sure of it. Tearing her gaze from the man who was her temporary husband, she saw the estate gardener giving her a knowing smile.

"Calvin. Yes. I mean, I did want to ask you something. I was wondering if you'd mind providing a few bouquets for the dance tomorrow night. No one's flowers are prettier."

"Happy to," the older man said. "Anything in particular?"

She shook her head. At the moment, she couldn't have discerned the difference between a rose and a weed anyway. "No, I'll leave that up to you."

"You're in charge of flowers, too?" Hunter grumbled.

"I'm helping." And why did she say that as if she were apologizing? She didn't owe him an explanation, and why did he care what she did anyway? In the few days he'd been home, he'd gone into town only that one day when they'd had their shopping expedition. The rest of the time, he remained here, at the house, as if he were…hiding?

Even as she considered that, she discounted it. Why would Hunter Cabot want to hide from the very town in which he'd grown up? He wasn't the kind of man to avoid confrontation or uncomfortable situations.

"Sure seem to do a lot of 'helping,'" he commented dryly.

"And it seems that you don't do enough," she countered, enjoying the quick spark of irritation she spotted in his eyes.

But she wondered why he was so determined to keep himself separate from the town and the people here. He would only be here another few weeks; then he'd be gone back to the Naval base, back to the danger and adventure he seemed to want more than anything. So why, then, wouldn't he want to spend what little time he had here seeing old friends?

She knew she'd be leaving at the end of the month, so Margie wanted to do as much as she could for the town she'd come to love.

So why didn't he love this place? He'd been raised here. He'd had family to love. A spot in the world to call his own. And he'd given it all up for the chance at adventure.

"Now," Calvin announced, interrupting her thoughts again, "I've got weeding to do." But before he left, he gave Hunter a quick look and said, "You remember what we talked about."

Then Calvin wandered off and Margie watched his progress through the lush, cottage-style garden. When the older man rounded the corner of the big house, she shifted a look to Hunter. "What did he mean by that?"

"Nothing." He muttered the one word in a deep, dark grumble. "It was nothing."

"Okay," she said, while wondering what the two men had been talking about before she'd stepped onto the patio. But one look at Hunter's shuttered expression told her that he wouldn't be clearing up that little mystery for her. So she said, "He probably thinks he's giving us a chance to be romantic in the garden."

"Probably," Hunter agreed and didn't look like he appreciated it.

"Calvin never stops to chat for long anyway," Margie said, coming down the stone steps to the edge of the garden.

"Yeah, I know. He's always preferred his flowers to people."

She stopped, bent down and sniffed at a rose before straightening again. When Margie saw Hunter's gaze lock briefly on her breasts, she felt a rush of something completely female and had to hide a small smile. Really, she was in serious trouble. She was beginning to enjoy the way Hunter looked at her, and that road would only lead to disappointment.

He didn't trust her. He made that plain enough every time they were together. But he did want her. That much she knew. Every morning, she woke up to the feel of his heavy leg lying across hers, his strong arm wrapped around her waist and pulling her tightly against his warm, naked body. And every morning, she lay there, quietly, enjoying the feel of him surrounding her, until he woke up, shifted carefully to one side of her and replaced the pillow wall between them.

Margie knew he didn't realize she was awake for those few brief, incredible moments every morning. And she had no intention of telling him, because he'd find a way to end them and she liked waking up to the feel of his body on hers. To that sense of safety she felt lying next to him.

Oh, God. She looked up at him saw those blue eyes go cool and distant and knew she was only making things more difficult for herself. There was no future here for her at all. Pretending otherwise was only going to make leaving that much harder.

"Why'd you come out here?" he asked, his voice low, his features strained. "Did you really want to talk to Calvin, or were you just following me?"

So much for daydreams. "Were you born crabby, or do I just bring it out in you?"

"What?" He scowled at her.

He probably thought he looked ferociously intimidating. But Margie had seen that look often enough that it hardly bothered her anymore.

"Crabby. You. Why?"

"I'm not crabby," he said and blew out a breath. "Hell, I don't know what I am." Shaking his head, he glanced across the garden and Margie followed his gaze.

The back of the house was beautiful. Late-spring daffodils crowded the walkways in shades from butter-yellow to the softest cream. Roses sent their perfume into the air, and columbine and larkspur dipped and swayed brilliantly colored heads in the soft wind off the ocean. It was a magical place, and Margie had always loved it.

"You really like it here, don't you?" he asked.

"I love it."

"I did too for a while." He turned and started along the snaking path of stepping-stones that meandered through the garden. Margie walked right behind him, pleased that he was finally talking to her.

"When I was a kid," he mused, "it was all good. Coming here. Being with Simon."

"Your parents died when you were twelve. Simon told me. That must have been terrible for you." She didn't even remember her parents, but she'd been told they'd died in a car accident when she was three. She'd give anything to have the few short years of memories of being loved that Hunter no doubt had.

"Yeah, they did." He tipped his head back to glance at the clouds scuttling across the sky before continuing on through the garden. "And I came here to live, and it was a good place to grow up," he admitted, now idly dragging the palm of his hand across a cluster of early larkspur. A few of the delicate, pastel blossoms dropped to the ground as they walked on. "The place is huge, so there was plenty of room for a kid to run and play."

"I can imagine." Though she really couldn't. Growing up in a series of foster homes, Margie had never even dreamed of a place like this. She wouldn't have known how.

As if he'd guessed where her thoughts had gone, he stopped, looked over his shoulder and asked, "Where are you from?"

"Los Angeles," she answered and hoped he'd leave it at that. Thankfully, he did.

Nodding, he said, "Coming from a city that size, you can understand how small Springville started to look to me."

"That's exactly what drew me in when I first moved here. When I answered the ad to become Simon's assistant, I took one look at Springville and fell in love." It was the kind of small town that lonely people always dreamed of. A place where people looked out for each other. A place where one person could make a difference. Be counted. But she didn't tell him all of that.

"I like that it's small. Big cities are anonymous."

"That's one of the best parts," Hunter said and gave her a quick, brief smile that never touched his eyes. "There's a sense of freedom in anonymity. Nobody gives a damn what you do or who your family is."

"Nobody gives a damn, period," she said quietly.

"Makes life simple," he agreed.

"Running off to join the SEALs wasn't exactly an attempt at simple and uncomplicated."

He laughed shortly. "No, I guess it wasn't."

"So, what were you looking for?"

"Why do you care?" He stopped, turned to look down at her and in his eyes there were so many shifting emotions that Margie couldn't tell one from the next. Then he spoke again, and she was too angry to worry about what he was feeling.

"Seriously, I get why you're doing this. Five million is hard to ignore. But why do you care when it's not part of the job description?"

She sucked in a gulp of air and felt the insult of his words like a slap. "I told you. I'm not doing this for the money."

"Yeah, you told me."

"But you don't believe me." That truth was written on his face.

"I don't *know* you," he countered.

Margie pushed her hair back from her face when the wind snaked the dark red curls across her eyes. Looking up at him, she found herself torn between wanting to kiss him and wanting to kick him. It was a toss-up which urge would win.

"Is it so hard for you to believe that I might love this place? That I might love Simon?"

"I just don't see what you get out of it beyond the money," he told her. "Unless it's hooking yourself to the Cabot name."

Understanding began to dawn as she noticed the tone of his voice. "Is that what this is about? Is that why you left? You didn't want to be a *Cabot?* Why? Is it so terrible to have a family? To be a part of something?"

His jaw clenched. She watched the muscle there flex as if he were biting back words fighting to spill out.

Finally he let them come. "In this town, yeah, it's hard to be a Cabot," he admitted. "Everybody looking to you to make sure they keep their jobs. Treating you like you're different. Figuring since you live in a castle, you're some kind of prince. I wasn't interested in being small-town royalty."

Margie laughed at that ridiculous statement. When he frowned, she held up one hand to cut off whatever he might say. "Please. I've heard plenty of stories about you when you were a kid, Hunter and in none of them did people talk about you like you were a prince. If anything, it was 'That Hunter was always into something.' Or 'Hunter broke so many of my windows I almost boarded 'em up.'"

A reluctant smile curved his mouth. "All right, I give you that. But..." He paused, looked around the postcard-perfect garden and then to the back of the castle, which seemed to glitter in the late-afternoon sun. "Simon wanted me to be the next link in the Cabot family dynasty. I wanted more. I wanted to be out in the world making my own mark. I didn't want to catch hold of the Cabot family train and ride on what my family's always done."

"So you walked away," she said softly. "From your friends. Your family."

She hadn't tried to mask the accusation in her voice, and he reacted to it. His spine went stiff as a rod, he squared his shoulders and looked down at her as if daring her to question his decisions. "What I do is important."

"I'm not arguing that," Margie said. "How could I? You risk your life for your country. For all of us. On a regular basis."

"Why is it I hear a 'but' coming?"

"*But,*" she said, accommodating him, "the smaller, less glorious battles are just as important, Hunter. The day-to-day work of building lives. Making people happy. Watching over the people you care about. That's no less honorable. No less significant."

"I didn't say that," he told her, his voice hardly more than a whisper of sound that seemed to slide over her skin like warm honey.

"Then why can't you see you're needed here?"

He shifted as if he were uncomfortable, and Margie hoped that she was getting through to him. As a Navy SEAL, Hunter knew his duty and did it, without question. Hadn't she listened to Simon talk with pride about the man Hunter had become? Hadn't she seen for herself since he'd been home how everyone treated him? The man was a hero. Now, she just had to make him see that this town—and Simon—needed their own hero back.

When she left, Simon would have no one again. Springville would slip back into the worry that without the support of the Cabots the town would die. Couldn't Hunter see that his family, his *home,* should now be taking precedence over his need for adventure?

He shifted his gaze from hers as if he couldn't look at her and say, "It isn't in my nature to stay."

Margie didn't believe that. She already knew he was a man who didn't avoid commitment. Hadn't he given everything to his country? "Then what is your nature, Hunter?"

"To protect." He said the words quickly. No hesitation at all. It was instinct. Turning his head, he gave her a hard, warning look, then added, "And I'll protect Simon from anyone trying to hurt him."

She knew exactly what he meant. He still believed that she was taking advantage of Simon. That she wanted only his money and whatever prestige came along with the name Cabot. He'd never understand that the love Simon had offered her had been far more valuable to her than dollars.

Suddenly she was tired of trying to make him understand. Tired of the veiled insults and the way he seemed to look at her with hunger one moment and disdain the next. If he was too hardheaded to see the truth, she'd never be able to convince him. And, since this farce would be over in a few weeks, why should she keep trying? Why should she keep beating her head against a stone wall when all she got for her trouble was a headache?

As he stood there watching her, waiting for her to try to defend herself yet again, Margie decided to take an offensive road rather than a defensive one.

"You want to protect Simon from anyone trying to hurt him? Like you did, you mean?" Margie's voice was quiet, but the words weren't. They seemed to hang in the air between them like a battle flag. "You left Simon alone, Hunter. You walked off to save the world and left an old man with no one to care about him."

His cool blue eyes went so cold, so glacial, that Margie wouldn't have been surprised to see snow start flying in the wind between them. "Didn't take you long to move in and correct that, though, did it?"

Anger swamped through her and rose like a tide rushing in to shore. Stepping in close, she lifted one hand, pointed her index finger and jabbed it at his chest. "I was his *employee*."

He glanced down at her finger, then wrapped his

hand around hers and pushed it aside. "So, you were doing it for the money. Still are, aren't you?"

Margie pulled her hand free of his and shook her head at him sadly. As quickly as her anger had risen, it drained away again. What was the point? She stepped back from him because she needed the physical distance to match the emotional chasm spreading between them.

"It would be easier for you if that were true, wouldn't it?" she whispered, forcing herself to look into those hard, cold eyes. "Because if I'm staying because I love your grandfather, that makes you leaving him even worse, doesn't it?"

"You don't know what you're talking about," he muttered.

"Oh, I think I do. You're a coward, Hunter."

"*Excuse* me?"

She waved a hand. "Don't bother using that military, snap-to-attention tone of voice with me. I'm not afraid of you."

"Maybe you should be," he warned. "Nobody calls me a coward."

"Really? What else would you call a man who turns from the only family he knows because it's just too hard to stay?"

He didn't say anything to that, and when the silence became too much to bear, Margie turned and left him standing amid the spring flowers.

And because she didn't look back, she didn't see Hunter watching her long after she'd disappeared into the house.

Six

The dance was a success.

But then it would have to be, Hunter thought. His "wife" wouldn't have settled for anything less.

To please his grandfather, Hunter was wearing his dress whites, and so he stood out in the crowd of dark suits and ties even more than he might have usually. Now, leaning one shoulder against the wall in a corner of the room, he tried to disappear as he watched the crowd assembled in a local church hall.

It was the only room except for the ballroom at the castle that was large enough to accommodate this many people. And from Hunter's vantage point, it looked as if most of the town had turned out for the event.

There were dozens of small round tables arranged around the room, with a long buffet line along one wall.

The dinner had been catered by a restaurant in town, and the tantalizing spices and scents of Mexican food hovered in the noisy air. There were helium-filled balloons trailing colorful ribbon strings bouncing against the ceiling, and Calvin's flowers decorated either end of the buffet table.

There was music blasting from someone's stereo at the front of the room, and several couples were on the dance floor swaying to the beat. But mostly, people wandered the room, laughing and talking as if they hadn't seen each other in years.

Then, there was his "wife," Hunter thought. His eyes narrowed on the redhead who'd done nothing but plague him for days. Since their conversation in the garden the day before, he hadn't been able to stop thinking about everything Margie had said to him, and that just irritated the hell out of him.

He didn't want to feel guilty. He didn't want her looking at him in disappointment as if he'd somehow let her, personally, down. He didn't want to remember her words and hear the ring of truth to them.

Oh, not the coward part. That he'd fight until his dying breath. He was no coward. He hadn't run from responsibility. He'd run *to* it. He'd wanted something different for his life. He'd wanted to leave a mark, to do something important. And he had. Damned if he'd apologize for that.

He straightened abruptly from the wall and felt a twinge of pain from his still-healing wound. And along with that ache came a whispering voice that asked, *Haven't you had enough of the adventure? Hadn't you already been thinking that maybe it was time to come home?*

Scowling out at the woman who'd made him think too much, remember too much, Hunter tried to brush her and all she stood for aside. But that was harder than he might have expected.

"You ought to be out there dancing with your wife," a deep voice said from somewhere nearby.

Hunter glanced to his left and smiled. "Kane Hackett." He shook hands with his old friend and said, "I don't dance. You should know that."

Kane grinned and slid a look across the room to where Margie was laughing and talking with a short blond woman. "A married man will do lots of things he didn't use to do. Take that gorgeous little blonde talking to your Margie…"

Hunter had hardly noticed the other woman. How could he be expected to see anything but how that strapless black dress Margie was wearing defined her lush body? Now, though, he forced himself to look at the blonde. "Cute."

"Damn sight better than cute," Kane corrected, taking a sip from the beer bottle he held. "That's my wife, Donna."

Staggered, Hunter looked at the man who had gone off to join the Marines at the same time Hunter had enlisted in the Navy. "You? Married?"

Hardly seemed possible. Hunter and Kane had both been keen on adventure, on seeing the world. Experiencing everything life had to offer and then some. Now Kane was married?

"Why sound so surprised?" His old friend chuckled. "You took the plunge, why not me?"

"Yeah, but—" Hunter's marriage was a fraud. "And you live here in town? Simon didn't say anything to me."

Kane shrugged. "Guess he was just waiting for us to bump into each other. And, yeah, I live in Springville. I'm the sheriff."

Hunter laughed now. "Oh, that's rich. You're the sheriff? After all the times we got hauled in for a good talking to, the people in this town elected you?"

Kane gave him a huge grin. "Guess they figured it took a bad boy to catch the bad boys."

Nodding, Hunter slid his gaze back to his wife as the music changed from classic rock and roll to a slow slide of jazz. "How long have you been back?"

"About a year and a half. Met Donna on my last leave. She knocked me off my feet, Hunt." He grinned and shook his head as if he still couldn't believe it himself. "Never saw it coming, but I'm glad it did." He paused then added, "So when my enlistment was up, I came home, ran for sheriff and married Donna."

"No more adventures for you, then, huh?" Hunter reached out, took his friend's beer and had a swallow.

"Are you kidding?" Kane laughed. "Every day with Donna's an adventure. Best thing that ever happened to me, I swear. But then," he said, reclaiming his beer, "I guess you'd know all about that."

"Yeah." Hunter watched Margie as an old woman stopped to talk to her, and his chest tightened as Margie gave the woman her complete attention along with a brilliant smile.

Briefly, he wondered what it would be like to actually

be married. To know Margie was his with the same surety that Kane felt about his Donna. Would he resent staying in Springville? Would he end up one day hating the town and the woman who had snared him?

Hunter frowned at the thought and had to ask himself if maybe Margie hadn't been more than a little right in everything she'd said to him the day before. Maybe he had been running from responsibility and disguising it with a different kind of duty.

"Well, good to see you," Kane was saying. "Stop by the station this week—we'll catch up. For now, I think I'll go dance with my wife."

"Right, right." Hunter nodded but barely heard his friend. He was too busy watching Margie as, one by one, everyone in the hall found the time to stop and talk with her, laugh with her, hug her. Something about that woman made her a magnet for people. Was it a con artist's gift, he wondered, or was it simply that she was a naturally kind person whom people wanted to be around?

"You know," Kane said, slapping Hunter on the back, "I really shouldn't even be speaking to you, all things considered."

"Huh? Why's that?"

"Because ever since Margie told Donna and some of the other wives about that honeymoon you two had in Bali…" Kane's eyebrows lifted and he huffed out a breath. "Well, let's just say, those stories made the rest of the husbands in town come in a sad second place to you in the romance department."

Bali, huh? So Margie was making up stories about honeymoons on tropical islands. And, painting him in a very romantic light, apparently. He smiled to himself and wondered just how detailed those stories had been.

"What can I say, Kane?" Hunter said with a slow smile. "I've always been good."

"That you have, Hunt." Kane slapped him on the shoulder again and walked past him. "You're missed around here, you know. It's good to have you back, man."

"Good to be back," he said automatically, but for the first time he realized he actually meant the words.

Margie felt Hunter's gaze on her as surely as she would a touch. Was he still angry about the things she'd said to him the day before? Not that he hadn't deserved it, she reminded herself while Jenna Carter babbled about the dessert tray. Margie nodded absentmindedly and remembered the way Hunter had looked at her when she'd called him a coward.

Even now, she cringed and wished that she'd found a better way to say what she'd meant. Yes, she thought he'd deserted Simon and the town that needed him, but she also knew he wasn't a coward. He was strong and sure of himself and brave and—*arrogant, bossy and irritating,* her mind added quickly before she became just a little bit too understanding.

After all, he hadn't exactly been kind to her. He was still convinced she was trying to scam Simon, for heaven's sake. At the thought of the older man, she shifted a quick look at him and spotted him sitting with his friends, laughing and whispering together. And men thought women gossiped.

Simon. She would miss him when she left. And God

help her, she would really miss Hunter. Somehow, that man had wormed his way into her heart, making her want him despite the fact that he thought she was a thief. *Margie, you are such an idiot,* she told herself.

Then Mrs. Banks murmured something about having a meeting the following month concerning the elementary school festival, and Margie only nodded. She wouldn't be there next month, and that knowledge was too painful to allow, so she buried that ache and let it simmer in the heat that Hunter's stare was causing.

How in the world was she going to make it through the rest of the night? Her insides were shaking, and her smile felt forced and wooden. She only hoped no one else could tell that her heart was breaking.

With Kane's words still repeating in his mind, Hunter left his corner and stalked the perimeter of the crowd. He nodded to those he passed, but he didn't stop. To stop meant being drawn into conversations, and he wasn't in the mood to talk. Not to old friends. Not to anyone. His thoughts didn't make him good company at the moment. Instead, he sought a darker corner, a quiet spot from which to watch and observe.

The music swelled around him, pulsing with an almost erotic beat, that slow, heavy sound of wailing sax that crept into a man's soul and wrung it dry.

He moved stealthily, using his training as a SEAL to help him slide almost unnoticed through a crowd so busy with their partying they didn't notice much of anything else. Across the room he spotted Simon—who'd decided to attend at the last minute—sitting at a table near the dance floor, holding court with some of his cronies. Old men gathered together to remember the past and plan for a future that most of them wouldn't see. A pang of something sharp and bitter sliced into him as he realized once again that his indomitable grandfather was old now. How much longer would he be here? How much more time could Hunter reasonably expect to have with the man who was his only family?

He clenched his jaw and deliberately shifted his gaze from Simon to Margie. As always, she was surrounded by a crowd, laughing and smiling as if she didn't have a disturbing thought in her head. But then, he thought, why would she? She'd dumped all of them on *him* the day before.

That he could acknowledge that just maybe he might have deserved some of her taunts only annoyed the hell out of him. His gaze fixed on her as she greeted all of the people who seemed to move in a stream toward her. She smiled, she laughed, she welcomed people into her warmth. People who weren't *him,* of course.

But when that thought scuttled through his mind, Hunter at least had the grace to admit that it was his own damn fault. He shut her out whenever his desire for her became too overwhelming—which was damn near every minute. He didn't want to care about her. Didn't want to want her. Didn't want to see beyond what he'd already seen. She was the manipulative woman he'd first thought her. She *had* to be because anything else was simply unacceptable.

They weren't really married. He'd made her no promises and didn't intend to, he reassured himself. When this month was over, he'd be leaving. Back to the Navy. Back to the next mission.

And who, his mind demanded, would be here to look after Simon?

The fierce scowl on his face that thought engendered was enough to convince most people to give him a wide berth, and Hunter was grateful for it. He was visited out. No more friendly chats tonight. All he wanted to do was survive this dance, get back to the castle and locate one of Simon's bottles of aged scotch.

At last, he found a slice of darkness, an alcove off the entrance, far enough away from the crowd that he could think without being interrupted by old friends. But close enough that his gaze could search out Margie. Damn it.

What was it about her that got to him? She was nothing like the women he was used to. She was…unlike anyone he'd ever known. God, when he compared her with his ex, it was as if the two women were from different planets.

Gretchen didn't want to think about tomorrow. She was the quintessential party girl. She was ready for adventure, good in the sack and beautiful enough to make a grown man whimper. But, he reminded himself, just two months before Hunter had hinted that he might be thinking about settling down. Maybe getting married—okay, no time soon, but someday. When he was too damned old to go out and get himself shot anymore. Gretchen had backed off like he was on fire and she didn't want to be singed by the flames. She'd broken up with him that night and taken off for a photo shoot in Peru, of all damn places.

Shaking his head, Hunter folded his arms over his chest, leaned back against the cold wall and watched

Margie. Unlike the gorgeous Gretchen, his temporary wife was all about the future. She was always planning tomorrows, looking ahead, dreaming dreams and finding a way to make them real.

Hell, she knew their marriage was a lie, yet she continued to pretend to everyone in town that all was well between them. She continued to do her best for a town that she was going to be leaving soon.

And she told sexy stories about him and a honeymoon that hadn't happened.

What the hell was he supposed to do with a woman like that?

Of course, he knew what he wanted to do. At least, what his body was clamoring for. But sex with Margie would complicate a situation that was already so twisted he couldn't see an easy way out. So he'd bury his lust and focus on getting through the next three weeks or so.

In the next instant, he wondered where Margie would go when she left Springville. What would she do? What would Simon do without her?

He rubbed one hand over his face and tried to wipe out the scrambling thoughts in his mind. But how the hell could he not think about her when she was there, in front of him, looking sexier and more desirable than ever?

"I never really believed Hunter was married to her," a woman said to her friend as she blithely walked past the shadowed alcove where Hunter stood silently.

"What do you mean?"

"Oh, come on." The first woman, a brunette who looked familiar to Hunter, laughed lightly. "I mean, when you look at Margie, do you really think…hmm, there's the woman for Hunter Cabot."

"I guess not," her friend said and shifted to look at Margie.

Hunter did too and frowned as the brunette kept talking.

"I knew him in high school, and even then he was the stuff dreams were made of."

He frowned and thought about moving out of the shadows so the women would know he was there. Then he second-guessed that idea. He'd learned long ago that a man could learn a lot with a little eavesdropping, so he held his ground and waited.

"I can imagine," the second woman said. "The man is…wow."

"Exactly. He's wow and she's…ho-hum. I mean, she's nice and everything—"

Nice? Margie was nice? Gritting his teeth hard, Hunter glared at the brunette. Margie worked continuously for this town, giving everything she had, and these two women felt comfortable standing in the shadows of the dance Margie had arranged and bloodlessly tearing her apart? Temper sparked and a protective surge like nothing he'd ever known before rose up inside Hunter.

"Completely," her friend agreed quickly. "Margie's a sweetie."

"But he's a…*god,* and she's a peasant. Never should have happened. And—" The brunette stopped, glanced at her reflection in a nearby window and smoothed her pinky finger over her bottom lip. Sighing, she said, "Until Hunter actually showed up here and claimed her, I never believed those stories she told all over town."

"Mmm," her friend said on a sigh. "Like Bali?"

"Yes..." The brunette shook her head, stared across the room at Margie and said, confusion ringing in her tone, "What the hell does she have that I don't have?"

"For one thing," Hunter spoke up and stepped out of the shadows, startling both women into gasping. "She's got *me.*"

"Hunter—I—we—" The brunette threw her friend a desperate look, but that woman was already melting into the crowd, disassociating herself fast.

He looked down into the brunette's eyes and finally placed her. Janice Franklin. Cheerleader. Homecoming queen. And still the town's reigning bitch, apparently.

"Janice, right?"

She brightened, obviously pleased to be remembered. "Yes."

Hunter just looked at her for a long minute or two. She was still pretty, in a hard, sharp way. And clearly, she thought highly of herself if she figured he'd just brush aside everything she'd said about his "wife" without a second thought. Well, she was wrong. He wasn't going to stand there and let this woman—or anyone else for that matter—sharpen her claws on Margie's hide. Why it mattered to him so much, he couldn't have said. All he was sure of was that it did matter. He'd worry about the why of it later.

"Well, Janice," he finally said softly, chucking her chin with his fingertips, "let me tell you something else about my wife. What she has someone like you will never understand."

She blinked at him. "Well—I—"

"Do yourself a favor," Hunter told her as he left her babbling to herself, "don't say anything else."

Riding a wave of righteous fury on Margie's behalf, Hunter stalked through the crowd. His gaze locked on his wife, he was like a ballistic missile, focused solely on his target.

Who the hell did those women think they were, talking about Margie as if she were less than nothing? As if she wasn't good enough for him? Good enough? Hell, if she was everything she claimed to be, she was too damn good for him. What right did they have to say a word about his *wife?*

The fact that he was inwardly defending the woman he'd been complaining about for days didn't register with him. His only thought now was to get his hands on her. To make sure everyone here understood that they'd better treat her right.

Across the room, Margie looked up and saw Hunter headed right toward her. He was hard to miss, she thought, with an inward sigh. In his white dress uniform, with the rows of colorful ribbons and medals on his chest, he looked like every woman's fantasy. He was tall and strong and fierce and…headed right for her with an expression on his face that was a mixture of fury and determination.

What was wrong? A woman beside her was talking, but Margie didn't hear a word. Instead, she was caught up in the power of Hunter's blue gaze locked on hers. The people separating them seemed to melt out of his way, propelled by some invisible force. Margie's heart pounded and her breathing hitched as he came closer, never slowing down, never hesitating.

What was going on? She'd hardly seen him all evening, though she'd been aware of him. How could she not be, she wondered frantically. The man was inescapable. Just knowing he was in the room had kept her on edge all night—wondering what he was doing, what he was thinking—had had her own mind racing, questioning.

Now, he was only an arm's reach away, and the only thing she read on his face was a strength of purpose she couldn't identify.

"Hunter—" She spoke first as soon as he stopped in front of her. "Is everything all right? Are you—"

"Quiet." It was a command no less authoritarian for its whispered delivery.

"What?"

Then Hunter shook his head as if not surprised at all she hadn't been able to be quiet. His lips curved into a wicked smile that sent a jolt of something amazing staggering through her. And before she could recover, he grabbed her, swept her into a low dip, cradled her in his arms and kissed her, so long, so hard, so deep, that Margie forgot to breathe.

His mouth on hers was at first wild, aggressive, almost as if he didn't want to be doing what he was doing. But she responded to that hint of darkness instantly, as if the shadows in this man had reached out and found every dark corner of her own soul. There was fire here, a ferociousness she hadn't expected but thrilled to, in the deepest corners of her heart. In seconds, his kiss changed, shifted, became less brutal, more hot and hungry, more passionate. Margie sighed into his mouth and felt his body mold itself to hers as if he were trying to hold her so tightly she'd never be able to escape him.

She didn't know what had prompted this, and she didn't care. Since the first time he'd kissed her, days ago, she'd been dreaming about another one. And this kiss more than lived up to her fantasies. Her blood felt like champagne, bubbling into a froth that swam giddily through her veins. His tongue swept into her mouth, stealing her breath, filling her with a heat that felt overwhelming, mind boggling.

She gave herself up to it, and when her mind started whispering, she resented every taunting thought. *What was he doing? Why was he kissing her? Was it all a show for the townspeople? And if it was, why now? Why tonight? He hadn't seemed to care if anyone believed they were married or not. So what had changed?*

And why do you care? that voice murmured at last. Did she really have to question this? Couldn't she just, for once, enjoy the moment? Feel his arms around her and pretend, however briefly, that they were a real couple? Couldn't she just convince her brain to take the night off and let her body lead the way?

Oh, yeah.

Lost in sensation, she wrapped her arms around his neck and gave him everything he was giving her. And while she surrendered to the heat, she was only dimly aware of the thunderous applause rising up from the people surrounding them.

Margie couldn't sleep.

How could anyone be expected to sleep when the bodies were simmering at a high boil and sexual expectation was humming along at a gallop? Hmm. Mixed metaphors. Probably a bad sign.

Apparently her "husband" wasn't feeling any lingering effects from that kiss. His deep, even breathing sighed into the silence, telling her that at least one of them was going to get some rest that night.

Jerk.

With the pillow wall at her back, Margie tried to ignore the fact that Hunter had been ignoring her for hours—ever since that spontaneous kiss had ended. As if he somehow was blaming *her* for him kissing her. And wasn't that just like a man? Right back to Adam in the Garden. *It was all that woman's fault.*

She punched her own pillow and shifted position, trying to find a spot where the sheets didn't seem to be scraping sensitive skin raw. Where she could hear the sound of Hunter's breathing and not imagine that breath dusting her face as he loomed over her.

Moonlight sifted into the bedroom through the French doors and lay in a silvery blanket across the bed. In the dim light, she stared up at the ceiling and told herself she'd never fall asleep if she didn't close her eyes. But then every time she closed her eyes, she felt Hunter's mouth on hers again, so no sleep that way, either.

She folded her arms over her chest, pinning the sheet and quilt to her body and tried silently repeating multiplication tables. Maybe she could bore herself to sleep.

That's when Margie noticed Hunter's breathing pattern had changed. She listened harder, noticed the quickened tempo of his breaths, as if he were running in his sleep, and she went up on one elbow to peer over the pillow wall.

He yanked a field dressing out of his pack and wrapped it around his side in an effort to stop the bleeding. Damn lucky shot, he told himself, fury at the situation spiking inside him.

Should have been a simple recon mission. But he'd been cut off from his team almost from the moment they entered the target area. They'd had to break for cover; then he'd been trapped, forced to hide while the others stealthily made a break for it.

The SEALs never left a man behind, and he knew his team would be waiting for him. They'd never evac the country without him, but it would be up to him to make it to the rendezvous point. Which would have been a hell of a lot easier if he hadn't been bleeding.

With pain his only companion, Hunter inched his way across a desert barren of any life but the enemy. He hid during the day, traveled at night. He rationed his water and was finally forced to dig the bullet out of his side with his own fingers. Days crawled past and tension, along with a fever, mounted. There were so many dangers, so many easy ways for him to die and be lost in this damn desert forever.

But he wouldn't go that way, he told himself. He'd find a way out. Get back to where things were green. Quiet. Where he didn't have to constantly expect the muffled explosion of a gunshot coming out of nowhere.

*He wanted...*In his sleep, Hunter heard a whisper of something soft, something comforting, and he turned toward it, instinctively reaching. *Warmth surrounded him. A gentle touch smoothed his hair back from his face* *and whispered words of comfort swam through his mind, his heart. He reached for the source of that calm, for the ease it promised, for the balm he so desperately needed.*

Gentle hands stroked his skin, and Hunter groaned at the sensation. He was back, he was out of the desert. It hadn't killed him, after all. And here he was, with a warm, willing woman sliding her hands over his back, tenderly across his face, and he wanted that touch more than he wanted his next breath.

Coming up completely out of the dreamscape he'd wandered through, Hunter heard that whisper again, and this time, he recognized the speaker.

"It's okay, Hunter," Margie soothed, while her hands stroked him tenderly. "You're okay. You're safe. Come back."

He took a slow, deep breath and drew her scent of jasmine deep into his lungs. His eyes cleared and he looked up into her grass-green eyes and felt something stir and shift inside him. The same something he'd fought all night after kissing her at the dance.

Well, he thought, staring up at her, feeling her hands on his bare skin, he was through fighting. He wanted her. Had wanted her for days.

And now he was going to have her.

Seven

Reaching up, he cupped the back of her neck in his palm and pulled her head down to his. The first taste of her inflamed him, jolting through his body like a zap from an electrical wire.

She stilled briefly, then groaned into his mouth and returned his kiss with an eagerness that staggered him. Hunter used one hand to shove the pillows separating them aside, then yanked her close, molding her cotton-nightgown-clad body tightly against him. Every curve, every luscious inch of her was molded to him; he felt her heat searing his skin, and he wanted more. He wanted *all*.

"Take this off," he murmured, moving his mouth a scant inch from hers.

"Yes, take it off. I want to feel you," she whispered,

her small, soft hands moving, constantly moving over his chest, his back, through his hair, scoring his scalp with her short, neat nails.

Every touch was fire. A blessing. A benediction. A compulsion. He wanted her skin beneath his hands. He wanted to trace every delectable curve with his fingertips, his mouth, his lips. He wanted everything she had to give, and then he wanted it again.

He raised himself up on one elbow, undid the buttons on that blasted gown—the very one that had been tempting him nightly—and then slowly, lingeringly, pulled the nightgown up and over her head. Her incredible hair fluffed out around her head as she lay back on the pillows, and he could think only about burying his face in the mass of curls, inhaling her scent, taking the tenderness she offered so openly.

Hunter had never felt anything like this. Such a wild, frenetic mixture of passion and gentleness. A driving need to bury himself inside her heat blended with the frenzied urge to watch her as she came. To push her higher and higher, to see desire flash and burn in her eyes, to hear her cry his name and feel her splinter in his grasp.

"You've been making me crazy for days," he muttered, dipping his head to take first one rosy nipple into his mouth and then the other.

"I have?" she whispered, then, "Ohh…"

"That nightgown of yours. Covering up what I knew was under there." He shook his head against her body, trailing his tongue around the edges of her nipple before nibbling gently at its peaked tip. "Ugliest, most seductive thing I've ever seen."

"I didn't know," she admitted, then arched up, pushing her breast into his mouth, silently asking, demanding more.

He gave it to her, sucking until she whimpered, while his hand swept down her lush body, sliding across jasmine-scented, soft, smooth skin, to the juncture of her thighs. He found her wet and hot for him and groaned himself as he cupped her, rubbing his hand over her center, loving how she lifted her hips into his touch.

"Hunter…"

Her breathy sigh filled the room and shuddered inside him. Hunter wanted her more than he'd ever wanted anything in his life. He'd never known such need, such all-consuming desire. And he wanted more.

Reaching quickly to the bedside table, he pulled the drawer open, rummaged one-handed inside it and came out with a condom. Quickly, he tore it open, tossed the foil wrapper and sheathed his aching body. Then he looked down at her, losing himself in her eyes. Moonlight played on her skin, making her flesh seem to shimmer in the pale wash of silver.

"Never get rid of that nightgown," he ordered, already imagining watching her wear it, knowing what was beneath it, being able to pull it off her, like unwrapping a much wanted present.

"Right. Never."

He grinned and slid closer, moving his mouth down now, across her rib cage, down to her abdomen to flick his tongue at her belly button. And still his hand worked her core. Fingers stroking, thumb pressing against the heart of her while she quivered and trembled for him like a finely played musical instrument.

He was the master, but she was the treasure. He touched her; she responded.

Her hands smoothed over his shoulders, her fingernails drawing light lines of sensation across his skin until he felt as if each one of her fingertips was a lit match head, singeing him down to the bone.

She carefully maneuvered around the bandage low on his hip and whispered, "I don't want to hurt you."

"You won't," he assured her, pausing for one kiss, then another. "I'm fine."

"Are you sure?"

The concern in her eyes touched him even more deeply than the flash of desire he read there as well.

"Let me show you," he murmured, and before she could speak, he had shifted position so that he kneeled before her, lifted her hips from the bed and covered her wet, slippery heat with his mouth.

He looked at her then, her green eyes wide with passion and dazzled with pleasure as she rocked into him, instinctively reaching for the release he didn't plan on giving her just yet. He took her to the edge again and again, working her flesh, driving her higher and higher. Her whimpered pleas became groans, and those became demands and still he wouldn't let her find satisfaction. He kept her on a razor's edge, even though he tortured himself as well.

His body hard, aching and unable to wait another minute, Hunter laid her down, covered her body with his and pushed himself deep into her heat. She was tight and hot and—gasping in shock.

"I don't believe it," he managed to say on a groan.

A long moment passed as he held himself still inside

her. He looked down into her eyes and saw pain melt into pleasure and forced himself to ask, "You're a *virgin?*"

She grabbed at him, her hands exploring his body so thoroughly he quivered under her touch. "Not anymore," she said.

"You should have told me." He was poised on the brink. So close to exploding that beads of sweat broke out on his forehead as he used every ounce of his self-control.

"Sex now, talk later," she told him firmly, then lifted her hips, taking him in deeper, farther, so that he had no choice but to lay final claim to her body. "I had no idea," she whispered, squirming beneath him. "This feels…amazing."

"It's about to get better," he said, damning himself. No way was he going to stop. Not when she so clearly wanted this as badly as he did. Besides, the damage was done. No going back now. But damned if he'd have her first time be so bloody quick. Easing back, he touched her center, where their bodies joined, and she jerked beneath him in surprise.

"That's it," he told her, watching as her eyes blurred, her mouth worked and her breath huffed in and out of straining lungs. Her hips moved beneath him and Hunter had to call on all of his discipline just to maintain. But he wanted her to explode first. He wanted to see it, to know that he'd touched her as deeply as she'd touched him.

He touched her, rubbed that one, most sensitive spot, with excruciatingly tender strokes, and when she at last surrendered to the power of her own climax, he took his hand away, gave a few hard, fast thrusts and erupted into a climax so powerful it left him shaking like a broken man.

When he collapsed atop her, he felt her arms come around him, cradling him to her. And wrapped in her tenderness, filled with her scent, Hunter dropped into a dreamless sleep.

"You should have told me," he accused when the first slice of sunlight slanted into the room.

Margie slowly opened her eyes, stretched languorously and looked up at the man hovering over her. "What?"

"About being a virgin," he ground out. "You should have told me.

Barely awake, her body still thrumming with the pleasures he'd shown her, Margie smiled. "Would you have made love to me if I had?"

He scowled at her. *"No."*

"Well, then," she told him, reaching to slide one hand across his broad, muscled chest, "I'm glad I didn't."

Of course she hadn't told him she was a virgin. It wasn't exactly something a twenty-nine-year-old woman would be eager to share. Especially since the reason she'd held on to it for so long was that she'd wanted to be in love when she had sex for the first time. Now *there* was something Hunter Cabot would have zero interest in knowing.

But it was enough for now that she knew. Margie was in love, despite the fact that there could be no happy ending in this for her. Her mind knew that she shouldn't fall, but her heart had taken the leap anyway. And there was no going back now. The deed was done. In more ways than one, she thought with an inner smile.

She could still feel Hunter's hands on her body, the smooth slide of his flesh joining hers. The taste of his mouth, the hard rush of his breath as he raced to join her in completion. It had all been so much more than she'd ever hoped. And well worth waiting for.

"Damn it, Margie." He caught her hand in his, holding it still. "Isn't this situation already complicated enough?"

She pulled her hand from his, pushed herself up onto her elbows and gave a quick glance down at her own body. She was still naked. Never had put her nightgown—that wonderful thing—back on. She felt slightly wicked, lying naked in bed beside a man who oozed sexuality from every pore. And that wicked thought produced a few others, tumbling through her mind with unrestrained glee. *Wow,* she thought, *unchain a virgin and then step back.*

But if she wanted more of what he'd shown her in the darkness last night, it was clear by the look on his face that she was going to have to do some convincing. With her newly discovered feminine power roaring to life inside her though, she told herself *no problem.*

"It doesn't have to be complicated, Hunter," she said, arching her back slightly, elevating her breasts with their hard, pink tips, closer to him.

His gaze darkened and his jaw clenched. Good signs.

"What're you—"

"We're *married,* Hunter," she reminded him, reaching out now to stroke her fingertips along his tight jaw until she felt that muscle relax under her caress.

Married. To the man of her dreams. The man who

would soon be leaving her, she reminded herself. Instantly, she shut down that particular train of thought. She didn't want to think about him leaving. She wanted to enjoy what she had now.

If there was one thing a foster kid learned early on, it was to live in the present. If you had a nice family, enjoy it while it lasted. If you had a present, treasure it. If you got an ice cream cone on a hot summer day, relish it. Because only God knew when—or if—something good might happen again.

"I'm your wife. You're my husband. Why shouldn't we…" She ran her hand down his neck, along his shoulder and down to one flat, male nipple. When she smoothed her fingertips across it, she was surprised—and pleased—to see him flinch at the sensation.

He trapped her hand under his, holding her palm to his chest, and Margie could have sworn she felt heat searing her skin from the contact. She loved touching him. Loved the feel of his hard, warm body under her hands. Loved knowing that she could push this incredibly strong man to the breaking point.

"It's asking for trouble, that's why," he told her, his gaze locked with hers, as if he could scare her off by looking especially intimidating.

It didn't work.

She lifted his hand, placed it on her breast and held it there. "It's not trouble I want, Hunter. It's you."

Margie watched him fight an inner battle and knew she'd won when his fingers moved on her breast, tugging at her nipple, rubbing the tip in quick strokes.

Shaking his head, he muttered thickly, "I want you, too. So God help us both."

He took her nipple into his mouth then and suckled her hard, deep, drawing on her breast as if his life depended on it. Margie sighed, arched into his mouth and bit down on her bottom lip as his mouth worked her tender skin feverishly. Her body trembled and quaked in eager response. She cupped one hand behind his head to hold him in place, loving the feel of his mouth on her. Loving what he could do to her with a kiss, a sigh, a touch.

Loving *him.*

Yes, she thought again, lowering her gaze to watch him suckle her, that was one thing she couldn't mention. And wouldn't. She loved him. This brash, arrogant, amazing man had stolen into her heart, and Margie knew she'd never get him out again. Knew she didn't want to.

Hunter wasn't interested in love, Margie told herself, even as his body and mouth took her back to that lush place of pure sensation. She knew he still didn't really trust her and was anxious for this month and their "marriage" to be over. A man like Hunter Cabot would never love a woman like her—their worlds were far too different for any kind of bridge to span them.

So Margie decided to do all she could to make the most of what time she had with him. She wanted all of the memories she could build in the next few weeks. She wanted to be able to remember with perfect clarity how it felt to have Hunter Cabot's hands and mouth on her.

She wanted the feel of his skin on hers imprinted on her mind so that it would never fade.

Reaching down, she curled her fingers around his

hard, thick body and felt a wash of heat fill her as he inhaled sharply. Sliding her fingers up and down his shaft, she felt the power inside him and wanted it inside *her.* How had she ever lived without knowing the feel of him. How would she ever live without him?

No.

She pushed that thought aside and reminded herself that now was the only important time. She squeezed gently, deliberately, and he hissed in another breath through gritted teeth.

"Now. Need you now," he murmured and pushed her over onto her stomach. His hands swept up and down her back, over her behind, cupping, kneading, and with every touch, Margie quivered like a too-taut bowstring about to snap.

Wicked, she thought wildly, turning her head on the pillow, feeling him slide his long, hard body over hers. Every caress fed the fires inside; every stroke of his fingers made her want more.

Then he lifted her hips, kneeled behind her and used his fingertips to open her for him. Her heat welcomed that first touch, and she whimpered his name as she closed her fists around the cool, silk sheets beneath her.

He pushed himself into Margie so deeply, so completely, that she gasped and shook with reaction. In this position, she felt so much more, felt him invade her higher and more fully than before. She pushed back against him as he rocked forward, and with every thrust, she felt him stake his claim on her more thoroughly.

Again and again, he pushed himself into her only to retreat and thrust harder the next time. She heard his breathing labor, felt his tension climb to the heights hers had reached, and still she wanted more of him. As he thrust into her, he leaned over her, braced himself on one hand and used the other to rub her center as his lips and tongue moved down her spine.

"Oh…my…"

When Margie's body shattered, dissolving into tremor after tremor of sensation, she cried out his name and was only dimly aware of him reaching his own release, while emptying himself into her depths.

Finally, Hunter rolled to one side of her, drew her in close and Margie snuggled into him, content in the circle of his arms. His breath dusted her hair, and she sighed, absolutely happy for the first time in her life.

"Better than Bali?" he asked.

Surprised, she tipped her head back to look up at him. "You heard about that?"

He grinned and her heart turned over. "Are you kidding? It's the first thing my friends ribbed me about."

"Oh, God. How embarrassing." She dropped one hand over her eyes, then peeked up at him from between her fingers. "At least I told everyone how good you were."

"Yeah." He chuckled. "Thanks for that. So, let's hear it. Was this better than Bali?"

He was teasing her. There was a light of humor in his eyes she'd never seen before, and Margie played along, enjoying this moment almost as much as she'd enjoyed the previous ones.

"Well," she said, "I'm not sure. After all, a man on his honeymoon goes all out. Now that you're just an old married man…"

He pulled her over to lie on top of him, then smoothed her hair back from his face with his hands. "You should know better than to challenge a Cabot."

An hour later, Margie was thoroughly convinced that Hunter Cabot was every bit as good in real life as he'd been on her fantasy honeymoon.

The next couple of weeks flew by.

Hunter slipped into a routine he hadn't seen coming and didn't really mind. He was used to being active and now that his wound was mostly healed, he saw no reason to change that.

Every morning before dawn, he tore himself from Margie's arms, left her sleeping in the bed that hadn't seen a pillow wall since that first incredible night together and went for a run.

The roads were familiar. He'd run them as a high school athlete, he'd run them to prepare for boot camp and he'd run them on those infrequent trips home since joining the Navy. He knew every field he passed, every house with lamplight just beginning to glow through the windows, every turn and curve in the road. It was all as familiar to him as his own face in the mirror.

In the silence, Hunter's mind was filled with thoughts he was normally able to dismiss or at least shove aside. But on narrow country roads, where his only company was the occasional bird sweeping across a brilliantly colored sky, there was too much time to think and no way to escape it.

He'd missed it here. For so long, he'd thought of Springville and the Cabot dynasty as a trap; he'd refused to allow himself to see the beauty of the place.

The near blissful *quiet.* He'd immersed himself in the adventure, the risk, the duty of a job he believed in, and had avoided all thoughts about the place that would always be home to him.

Now, though, this place was calling to him so deeply that the call to adventure was muffled inside him.

And time was almost up.

Soon, he'd be returning to base. Back to the job that had been his life for more years than he cared to think about. Since he was recovered, he would be assigned to missions with his team again, and as that thought registered, he waited for the rush of adrenaline-tinged expectation he always felt.

But it didn't come.

Frowning, he kept running, the sounds of his footsteps like a disembodied heartbeat thundering out around him.

It was Margie, he told himself. He'd allowed himself to be drawn into an affair he'd known from the first would be nothing but a mistake. And yet he couldn't really regret it, even now. Even knowing that he'd be leaving, a divorce would be filed and he would, most likely, never see her again.

His scowl deepened and his pace quickened. His breath charged in and out of his lungs, and sweat rolled down his bare back. Where would she go? What would she do? And how would he ever know if she was all right?

"Of course she'll be all right," he muttered, disgusted with himself. "She'll have five million reasons to be all right."

There. Reminding himself that she was doing this for the money made him feel less like a bastard for using her. Because, really, who was using whom?

He didn't even hear the car come up behind him until it paced him. Hunter didn't stop, just smiled at the man rolling down his window to talk to him. "Morning, Sheriff."

"Can take the man out of the Navy, huh?" Kane Hackett said with a grin. "Figured I'd find you out here running. You always did like this road for training."

Hunter kept going, sparing his old friend a derisive glance. "And it figures that you're driving the road, not running it. Out of shape, are we?"

One dark eyebrow winged up. "Not so's you'd notice."

"Then why are you here?"

"Have to go see Simon," Kane said, his smile fading into a worried frown. "Figured it'd be best if you were with me when I did."

That got Hunter's attention. He stopped running, bent in half and took a few deep breaths before asking, "What's going on?"

"There was a fire at the Cabot building in town last night," Kane said.

"Fire?" Hunter grabbed the edge of the car window. "Anyone hurt?"

"No." Kane shook his head. "The night cleaning crew went in; apparently one of 'em turned on a stove in the break room to make some tea. Left a towel too close to the burner."

"Damn it."

"That about covers it." Kane waved him over to the passenger side door. "There's damage to the first two floors, though, and I thought, well, Simon had the heart attack last year—"

Hunter was already moving. He climbed into the black-and-white SUV, buckled his seat belt and told his friend to drive.

"Well, how bad is it?" Simon wanted to know an hour later. The old man wore a faded blue robe, and his white hair was standing out around his head like cotton swabs on end.

"Kane took me by to see it for myself before he brought me back here to tell you," Hunter said, remembering that Kane had left right after delivering the news, leaving it up to Hunter and Margie to watch out for Simon's blood pressure.

Now as Margie poured Simon's coffee, Hunter watched his grandfather warily for any sign the old man was going to clutch his chest and drop like a rock.

"*And...*?" Not dropping. Instead, the old man wanted answers, not coddling.

Hunter gave him a wry grin. Apparently, Simon was a lot tougher than any of them knew. "And, it's a mess. The fire chief says no structural damage, but there's plenty of smoke and water damage to make up for it. Most of the files are on the upper floors, so that's good. We didn't lose much."

One corner of Simon's mouth tilted upward. "No," he said slowly, "I guess *we* didn't."

"Simon..." Hunter sighed. "That's not what I meant."

"Freudian slip, huh?" Simon looked pretty pleased for a man who'd just been told his company headquarters had nearly burned down.

Hunter hadn't meant "we" the way Simon had taken it. After all, the company wasn't his baby. He was a SEAL. But touring through the damaged building with Kane at his side, Hunter had actually caught himself thinking about the reconstruction. And what changes might be made. After all, if they were going to have to do some remodeling, there was no reason they couldn't do some updating as well.

Such as, for instance, making the break room larger. The area was so small now that it would comfortably hold only two or three people. The day care center Margie had instituted also had been ruined, since the room set aside for it was on the ground floor. Now that they were redoing it, he thought they should make it more kid friendly than the old room had been.

And the workers' cubicles that were now twisted and melted should simply be tossed. Why lock people away into separate little stalls? It's not as if cubicles gave people the sense of having their own little offices. All they really did was separate them from their coworkers, and what was the point in that?

"Hunter?" Simon prodded, "What're you thinking?"

What *was* he thinking? Scraping one hand across the top of his head, Hunter muttered, "Nothing. No thanks, Margie. No coffee." He put out one hand to stop the cup she held out to him. "All I want now is a shower."

Then he left the room fast before his own thoughts could start marching in time with Simon's.

"Well, well, well. Did you hear him?" Simon chuckled and took a sip of coffee that was mostly 2 percent milk.

"He doesn't want to stay, Simon," Margie told him.

"Nothing you can say will change his mind. You know that."

The old man's white eyebrows lifted high on his forehead and wiggled around like two worms on hooks. "It's not what *I* can say that'll keep him here, Margie, honey—it's you. I've seen the way he looks at you. And don't think I haven't noticed that you're looking *back.*"

"Simon, don't play Cupid," she warned, not wanting the man she loved like a grandfather to be as heart-broken as she was going to be when this all ended.

He only chuckled again. "You'll see…"

She sighed, took a sip of her own coffee and slumped back into the chair closest to Simon's. Margie had seen the *hunted* expression in Hunter's eyes before he left the room and knew that he was already regretting getting as involved as he had in the fire investigation. He didn't want the life that was waiting for him here in Springville.

He didn't want her.

Not beyond the tumbled hours they spent together in his bed, anyway. There at least, she knew he wanted her. Felt it in his every touch, his kiss. In the way he held her during the night and the way he turned to her when nightmares plagued him. But she also knew that at the end of the month, he would leave and let her walk out of his life.

Just acknowledging that sent a spear of pain darting through her heart, and Margie didn't know how she would survive when that pain was her constant companion.

Eight

Hunter didn't mind helping out, he told himself a few days later. After all, he was here, wasn't he? And there was just so damn much to do. There was the construction at the company headquarters to look after, and there was Simon's birthday party. Since Margie couldn't really be expected to do it all, and since he didn't have a clue about how to arrange a blowout party, Hunter had taken over the work on the building in town.

He met with the contractor, talked to the employees to get their ideas and helped to draw up plans for the remodeling. Now, sitting in Simon's study, with blueprints spread out in front of him on the desk, he asked himself how he'd managed to get sucked so far into the life of the town.

His grandfather was upstairs, taking a nap, Margie

was off in the kitchen talking to Simon's cook about the caterer's party menus and Hunter was sitting behind the very desk he'd spent most of his life avoiding.

"So, how'd you get here?" he muttered and poured himself a glass of scotch.

"We turned left into that freeway out front you call a driveway," a familiar voice said, answering the rhetorical question Hunter had posed.

"As long as you're pourin', brudda," another voice told him, "get two more glasses out."

Only one man Hunter knew used island slang in every conversation just to make sure people knew he was a proud, full-blooded Hawaiian. Hunter was grinning as he stood up to face two members of his SEAL team. Jack Thorne, "JT," his team leader, and Danny "Hula" Akiona were standing in the open doorway of the study.

"Where'd you guys come from?" Hunter asked as he came around the desk, hand out to welcome his friends.

JT was tall and blond with sharp blue eyes that never missed anything. Hula was just as tall, with black hair, black eyes and a smart-ass outlook on life. Damn, Hunter'd missed them both.

"We were on our way up to Frisco for a little R and R," Hula was saying. "Thought we'd stop and see how you were healing up. Didn't know we'd find you sitting in a mansion."

Hunter winced. Exactly why he'd never told his friends about his background.

Hula sniffed the air, then slid his gaze to where the decanter of scotch sat on the edge of the desk. "Hmm. Thirty years old. Single malt."

Hunter laughed. "How the hell do you do that?"

"It's a gift." Hula shrugged, looked around the immense study, then shifted a look back at his friend. "So how come you never told us you were stinkin' rich?"

JT frowned at him. "Nice. Real subtle."

"I don't do subtle," Hula told him and shifted a pointed look at Hunter. "Takes too long, life's too short. Gotta wonder why a friend keeps a secret like this, though."

Hunter blew out a breath. "So I wouldn't have to listen to you saying things like 'stinkin' rich.'"

"No offense, you know?" Hula glanced around the big room again, then slid his gaze back to Hunter. "Just surprising finding out one of our own is a gazillionaire."

"Shut up, Hula," JT said and walked into the study, his gaze also darting around the room, taking it all in.

"Have a seat," Hunter said, glad to see his friends despite the fact that they now knew his secret. He retrieved the scotch, got two more glasses and then sat down across from two of the men he routinely trusted with his life. They were looking around as if they couldn't believe what they were seeing, and he couldn't really blame them.

In all the time they'd been together, Hunter had never once mentioned that his family was rich. He hadn't wanted them or the others on the team to treat him differently. All he'd wanted was to be one of them. To be accepted for who he was, not what his family had. Now, though, he had to wince. Had to look to his friends as if he'd been lying to them for years.

Because he had been.

JT braced his elbows on his knees, stared at him and asked, "So why'd you never say anything?"

"Yeah, brudda," Hula said, his dark eyes flashing. "Seems you like to keep secrets, huh? What's wrong? Afraid I'll borrow money after one of our poker nights?"

Hunter sprawled in the chair, balanced his glass of scotch atop his flat abdomen and shot first one man, then the other, a hard look. "This is why I never said anything. You're both looking at me like I'm a rich sonofabitch."

"It's only the rich part that's new," Hula told him with a wink. "Seriously, man, why'd you hide it? If I had a great place like this, I'd be telling everybody."

"Yeah," JT said with a shake of his head. "We know. But then, you tell everybody you meet every minute of your life story."

"Well, I'm a fascinating man," Hula said with a smile before he took a sip of scotch. "Like the time I tangled with a tiger shark off the coast of Maui…"

"We already heard it," Hunter and JT said together.

Then the three of them grinned at one another like loons. And just like that, things were back on an even keel. The secret of his family's money was out, and his friends had put it aside already. Made Hunter wonder what the hell he'd been worried about for so long.

"I actually missed you guys," Hunter told them.

"Good to know," JT said, easing back into the leather chair. "When we didn't hear from you, I started thinking maybe you were reconsidering coming back to the team."

"I told him that was cracked," Hula said after a long,

appreciative sip of scotch. "No way Hunter doesn't come back, I said. Hell, Hunt *lives* for the buzz, man."

The buzz. What they called the adrenaline-laced rush they got just before a mission. What they all felt when they were given orders to complete and dropped behind enemy lines. What they celebrated when they were all back home safe.

The buzz had a hold on Hunter, and he couldn't deny it, but lately he'd been asking himself if the buzz was enough to live on. And how much longer could he do this job to the degree of perfection he expected of himself? He wasn't getting any younger, and already two or three of the guys he'd entered SEAL training with had retired or taken on stateside training jobs.

JT was rolling his glass of scotch between his palms and watching him quietly.

"What?"

"Nothing," his boss said. "You just seem…different, I guess."

"I'm not," Hunter assured him and wondered silently if he was trying to convince JT or himself. Because the truth was, everything had changed. In town. Simon. Margie. But had he? No, he told himself firmly, squashing the very idea. "Nothing's changed."

"Hunter?"

All three men whipped their heads around to face Margie when she entered the room. And then all three quickly stood up.

She was surprised and had stopped just inside the room. She wore a pale yellow, short-sleeved blouse over her favorite jeans and brown sandals on her small, narrow feet. Her hair was windblown into a tangled mass of curls that made a man want to run his fingers through them, and her green eyes were wide in embarrassment. "I'm sorry. I didn't know you had company."

"It's okay," Hunter said, glancing from her to the friends, who were looking at her with clearly admiring gazes. A flicker of irritation came to life inside him as he saw Hula give her a smile that had won him countless women over the years.

Hunter felt a stab of territorialism that surprised the hell out of him. But damned if Hula was going to make a move on his wife, right in front of him.

He didn't stop to ask himself if this was another secret he should keep. Why introduce her as his wife when he knew damn well there was a divorce hovering on the horizon? Because he didn't want Hula looking at Margie like a hungry man eyes a steak. Because she looked wide eyed and uncertain what to do and Hunter didn't want her to feel uncomfortable. Because, damn it, for right now anyway, she was *his.*

"Come on in, Margie. I want you to meet these guys." When she was close enough, Hunter draped one arm around her shoulders. "Jack Thorne, Danny Akiona, this is my wife, Margie."

JT grinned, clearly stunned. "Nice to meet you."

Hula coughed. "Your *wife?*" Shooting a look at Hunter, he said, "Man, what happened to Gretch—"

JT shoved him and said, "Sorry, Hula. I make you spill your scotch?"

Hula wiped the liquor off his black T-shirt and glared at his team leader. "No problem."

Margie looked confused, then smiled at both men.

"It's nice to meet Hunter's friends. Can I get you anything? Food? Coffee?"

"No, ma'am," JT said quickly. "Thank you, though. We just stopped for a quick visit. Then we're heading into the city."

"You sure you're his wife?" Hula asked, stepping away from JT before there could be another "accident."

Margie grinned. "I'm sure."

"That's too bad," he said with a slow shake of his head.

"Well." Margie backed up a step or two, turned for the door and said, "I'll let you visit. It was nice to meet you both."

Hunter watched her walk away, and despite his best intentions, his gaze dropped to the sway of her hips in those worn denim jeans she preferred. It didn't help any to finally look at his friends and see that Hula had been enjoying the same view. Irritation clawed at him.

"What the hell were you thinking bringing up Gretchen?" Hunter whispered when Margie was gone.

"Hey, man," Hula said in his own defense, "I was surprised is all. I mean, last time I heard, you were dating this Swedish goddess—now you're married to somebody else."

Hunter shot a look at the empty doorway and wondered if Margie had caught Hula's slip or if JT had managed to shut him up in time. And why the hell did he care if she knew about Gretchen? He and the model weren't together anymore. Besides, it wasn't like he and Margie were *really* married. He didn't owe her an explanation. So why, then, did he feel like a cheating husband who'd been caught in the act?

"So nothing's changed, huh?" JT asked.

"That's right," Hunter told him, knowing he didn't sound convincing. Hell, how could he?

"You know," Hula mused, "I like this one a hell of a lot better than Gr—" He stopped, covered his glass with the top of his hand to prevent spillage and stepped back from JT. "That other one, she was cold, man. Sort of empty. This one…" He smiled and nodded. "She's a different story."

Yeah, she was, Hunter thought, rubbing the back of his neck as he tried to ignore the rattle and clang of thoughts and notions running through his mind. Despite wanting to keep an emotional distance between him and Margie, she had gotten to him. She'd sneaked beneath his defenses and had managed to make him question the way he lived his life. Forced him to look at his decisions. His—

JT just looked at him for a long moment or two. Then thoughtfully, he said, "You know, you wouldn't be the first of us to choose to stay with his wife rather than risk his life every other day."

True. He'd seen plenty of other guys fall in love, get married and leave the military. But their situations were different. They were in love with their wives. He was deeply in lust. But he couldn't admit to more than that. If he did, too much in his life would be affected.

"I told you, boss," Hunter said tightly. "Not gonna happen. I'll be back. My…marriage won't stop me."

"Don't get me wrong, Hunt. I'm glad you're coming back, and we all know the buzz is good, man," Hula said quietly. "But you have a woman who loves you? That's a buzz, too."

Did she? Love him? He thought about that and wondered. Or, he asked himself, was she just enjoying him as he was enjoying her? Was she trying to make him need her? Was she hoping that he'd make this marriage a real one? And why was he thinking about all of this anyway? He knew what he had to do. What he always did. His duty.

"Not the kind I need," Hunter told him. "So why don't we quit talking about my wife and you guys tell me what's been happening while I've been gone."

They sat down again, and while his friends talked and filled him in on life on base, Hunter's mind drifted. He wasn't sure why. He should have been hanging on the guys' every word about the base and the other teams. Should have been eager to turn his mind back to his job, back to the world he'd sought and built. Instead, his gaze slipped to the doorway through which Margie had disappeared, and his mind filled with thoughts of her. How she looked, the scent of her, the sound of her laughter and even the soft whisper of her sighs.

She was more than he'd expected, more than he'd wanted, and playing this dangerous game of theirs was getting more complicated. Now he was lying to his friends about her, and they'd no doubt have questions when he and Margie got their divorce, too. He never should have agreed to this insanity.

Because there was a part of him that was buying into it. A part of him sliding almost effortlessly into the rhythm of married man. Of *Margie's* man. And that couldn't happen. Because his life wasn't here. No matter what Simon or Margie might want.

He'd be going back to the Navy because that was where he'd always felt he belonged. His friends, his team. The missions. He'd signed on to do a job and he would continue to do it. He'd given his word, and he knew what that entailed. He belonged to the Navy, not this little town.

But for the first time, that call to adventure seemed a little less compelling than it once had. For the first time, a part of Hunter felt that he would be leaving behind something important when he left.

Margie stood outside the open study doors and listened to the three men talk.

There was laughter and the rumble of deep voices, and she hugged herself as she picked Hunter's voice out of the crowd with ease. He sounded happy as he sat and talked about missions and danger and adventure, about the bonds that tied the men together.

This was something she couldn't fight. These men who were closer to Hunter than brothers had a hold on him that was so deep it couldn't be defeated. Even if she were trying to.

She knew that no matter how she wished things were different between them, Hunter would never stay with her. Even if he actually loved her—which he didn't—he still wouldn't stay. He was a SEAL, and she doubted that would ever change.

And just who was Gretchen?

A few days later, Hunter was feeling just as itchy as he had when his team members had visited. He felt as though he should be doing *something,* but he couldn't figure out exactly what. He worked out at the local gym, did his morning runs down country roads and in general tried to get back into shape for his return to duty.

But through all of it, a different kind of duty kept rearing its head, demanding he take notice. Over the last few years, when he'd come home to see Simon, he'd made fast visits, in and out and back to base. But this time, with his medical leave and Simon's precarious health and Margie, the visit had been a longer one. Long enough to remind Hunter that there was a world outside the Navy, that there were other duties every bit as important as the one he owed to his country.

And Hunter was having a hard time reconciling what he wanted to do with what he knew he *should* do.

"Hunter. Good. I was looking for you." Simon walked into the study, and his steps were slow and careful.

Hunter stood up to help, but the older man irritably waved him off. "I'm not helpless yet," he muttered, walking around the edge of the desk to pull out the bottom drawer.

His heart fisting in his chest, Hunter watched his grandfather and tried to tell himself that despite appearances, the old man was as tough as any SEAL recruit. There was steel in that old man's bones, he thought with pride. But even as he thought it, he knew that his grandfather wasn't as strong as he'd once been. That the years had taken a toll that Hunter had never allowed himself to notice before now.

Had he really been so selfishly determined to live his own life on his own terms that he'd avoided noticing how much Simon needed help? Was he really ready to turn his back on his grandfather? After all the elderly man had been to him? What the hell kind of man would that make him? Choose duty to country over duty to family?

Shaking his head, Hunter pushed away the thoughts crowding his mind, because he didn't have any answers. Instead, he concentrated on what his grandfather was doing. In the bottom drawer there were dozens of files, neatly arranged. While Hunter watched, Simon quickly thumbed through them all until he found the one he wanted. Then he set the file onto the desk and flipped it open. "I want you to look these over and sign them before you go."

Hunter lifted one eyebrow. "Getting me another wife?" he asked wryly.

"Wouldn't waste my time," Simon snapped. "You don't have the sense to appreciate the one I already got you."

The hell of it was, Hunter *did* appreciate Margie. Too damn much.

"Simon…"

"I'm not here to talk about Margie, boy. This is something else."

"What?" Wariness crept into his tone. Lamplight speared up from the desk, illuminating Simon's face from beneath, giving the older man an almost eerie look. Shadows crept over his eyes, and every line and crevice on his face was deeply defined.

Simon straightened up, looked his grandson square in the eye and said, "I'm turning over the family business to you."

"Damn it, Simon," Hunter said, lifting both hands as

if to ward the other man off. "Even if I wanted to take over, I've got seven more months on my enlistment. I won't be here."

"You can do most of the work through power of attorney, and I can keep an eye on things until you come back."

Hunter stood up, moved away from the desk and walked to the wide window that overlooked the acre of tidy green lawn and perfect flower beds. A colorful sunset was spreading across the sky and lengthening shadows from the row of trees at the edge of the yard. The road was lying beyond those trees, the road Hunter had taken so long ago when he'd made his bid for freedom. Strange now that the same road had brought him back. And wasn't he turning into a damn philosopher all of a sudden?

"That is," Simon added, "if you plan on coming back."

Hunter threw the older man a look over his shoulder and saw the expectation, the damn hope shining in his eyes even in the dim light of the study. And Hunter knew he couldn't fight it anymore. Knew that the only way he'd ever be able to live with himself was to accept the duty that had been waiting for him since childhood.

He knew too, at some deep-seated level, that this is how it was meant to be all along, what he'd been headed toward all his life, despite his attempt to avoid it. Maybe, he told himself, he'd had to go away to see where he really belonged.

"I'll come back, Simon."

A delighted smile creased his grandfather's face, and for one brief moment Hunter actually did feel like the hero he'd always wanted to be. Then reality crashed down. If he was going to be leaving the SEAL and coming home to stay, there were plans to set in motion, decisions to make. And he had to talk to Margie, he told himself.

The old man clapped his hands together and scrubbed his palms against each other. "I knew you'd do the right thing, boy. Eventually."

A wry smile curved Hunter's mouth. "Thanks. I think." Then he shoved one hand across the top of his head and rubbed the back of his neck. "I still have to go back to the base at the end of the month."

"Understood."

Hunter nodded, turned to face Simon and pulled in a deep breath. Finally, the tension in his chest had loosened. For days now he'd been torn about what to do. Questioning his own loyalties, feeling the tug of home and duty fighting with the call to return to the life he'd built. He'd been engaged in a silent battle within himself, and now that a decision had been made, he could breathe easy.

Yes, it would be hard leaving the Navy, but he was needed here. And, as he felt a slight twinge in his side, he reminded himself that he'd been thinking about the possibility of retirement ever since he'd been shot. So, maybe this was how it was supposed to be.

"What about Margie?"

Hunter focused on his grandfather. "What about her?"

"Well," Simon said, "if you're going to stay, there's no reason for her to go either, is there? You're already married. And I've seen the way you look at her, boy. I'm old, not blind."

He hadn't had time to consider all the options here. He'd just this minute decided to retire, for God's sake. It's not as if he'd thought everything through. But now that he did think about it, he wondered if Simon wasn't right. But, "We agreed to divorce."

"Damn hardheaded—"

Hunter wasn't willing to budge. He'd make up his own mind about Margie—without well-meant interference. "Simon, don't push it. Whatever happens between me and Margie is up to us, not you."

"She makes you happy, Hunter. Or hadn't you noticed that?"

Happy. With a wife he hadn't chosen. With a wife he'd suspected for too long was nothing more than a scam artist out for whatever she could finagle out of a lonely old man.

With a woman who set him on fire with a touch.

But damned if he'd let his grandfather run his personal life, too. "You can't screw with people's lives, Simon. You can't arrange everything the way you want it."

"Don't see why not, when I can see perfectly clear what should happen," Simon muttered.

"Because *you* don't get to decide my life, Grandfather. And you sure as hell don't get to decide Margie's." He loved the elderly man, but damned if he'd fall into line just because Simon demanded it. And if this was a sign of how things were going to be once he came home and took over the family business at last, then they were in for quite a few battles.

So, Hunter decided, it was best to stand his ground right from the get-go. "Back off of this, Grandfather."

"You look me in the eye and tell me you don't care for that girl," Simon challenged.

Well, that was the trouble, Hunter thought, as he deliberately looked away. He didn't know what the hell he was feeling at the moment.

Nine

After leaving his grandfather, Hunter immediately made the phone call he never would have believed he'd be making. Punching in the numbers from memory, he dialed JT's cell phone and waited in the garden while it rang.

"Thorne," the voice on the other end of the line suddenly snapped.

"Boss, it's Hunt." Hunter stared up at the cloud-swept sky, tipped his face into an ocean breeze and closed his eyes.

"Yeah, I know. What's up?"

What isn't? Hunter took a breath, opened his eyes and stared out at the broad expanse of lawn and garden. This was his home. And though he'd avoided the knowledge for years, this was his *place.*

"I wanted you to know," Hunter said, his voice ringing

with the steel and strength of his conviction in the decision he'd made, "I'll be coming back to base, but when my enlistment's up, I'm going to be leaving the team."

There was a long pause and then a soft laugh. "If you're waiting for me to be surprised, don't bother," JT said at last.

Hunter laughed then, a short, sharp bark of sound. "Well hell, boss. It surprises *me.*"

"It shouldn't, Hunt. You've got a life to go back to now. That wife of yours deserves better than a part-time husband."

Margie. She was a part of this decision, no doubt. How big a part was something Hunter hadn't let himself figure out yet.

"Yeah, I guess she does," he said because it was easy and it was a reason JT would understand. "Look, I don't like leaving the team in the lurch, so I wanted you to know so you could start looking into my replacement."

"Nobody's gonna be able to replace you, Hunt," JT told him. "But I appreciate it. We'll talk when your R and R is over, okay?"

Hunter scraped one hand across his face and nodded, though his friend couldn't see the action. "You bet. See you in a few days."

When he hung up, Hunter stood in the swath of sunshine and waited for regret to claim him, waited for the feeling that he'd made a mistake to slam home. But it didn't come. Instead, he felt a sense of peace he hadn't felt in a long time. Then he turned and looked up at the big house behind him. As if he sensed her presence, Hunter's gaze locked on the bedroom window.

"One more conversation to have," he told himself and stalked across the stone patio, determined to finish setting his life on its new course.

Margie was in the bathtub when Hunter went upstairs after getting off the phone. He saw steam wafting from the open bathroom door and heard the splash of water and her soft voice humming a little off-key. Even as his body went stiff and eager, his mind chided him, reminding him just what he'd come to see her about.

Now that he'd made the decision to take on the family responsibility, he and Margie had to talk. Damned if Hunter wanted to admit it, but Simon had a point. If Hunter was going to stay, there was no reason for Margie to go.

Nodding to himself, he stalked across the room, stepped into the bathroom and leaned one shoulder against the doorjamb. With her back to him, she sat in the dark blue, oversize spa-jetted tub, one arm draped across the edge of the tub, jasmine-scented bubbles floating on top of the water, caressing the mounds of her breasts. The tips of pink nipples poked through the water and his body reacted instantly. He had to shift position to ease the discomfort in his jeans—which only told him that continuing this "marriage" was a good idea. They'd already proven they were more than compatible in bed. She loved Simon and this town. Hell. She was happy here. Why wouldn't she want to stay?

Smiling to himself, he tore his gaze from the delectable sight of those twin nipples and said, "Margie?"

"Whoops!" She shrieked, slipped lower under the water and flipped her head around to stare at him, eyes wide. "God, Hunter! Are you trying to kill me?" She slapped one hand to her bubble-covered chest and added, "And if you are, could you *not* do it in the bathroom? Jeez, first in the shower, now in the bath. I really don't want to be found dead *and* naked."

He was smiling. Damn it, he usually ended up smiling around Margie. Hadn't really thought about it before this moment, but Simon was right. She did make him happy. When she wasn't making him crazy in bed. She was fun to talk to. Easy to be around. She'd made him realize there was more in his life to think about than his own ambitions. She wasn't afraid to stand up to him, either, and he liked that. He liked *her.*

Plus, the sight of her naked body turned him into a pillar of fire, burning up from the inside out. All good things.

Hunter watched as she pushed herself higher up against the back of the tub, and his gaze dropped to her breasts, almost completely exposed by the disappearing curtain of bubbles.

His body went even harder than it had been before, and Hunter fought down a groan. Hell, he told himself, get the talking with over—then he'd join her in that soapy water and show her a few things with the tub's jets.

"Is everything all right?" she asked, smoothing a wet washcloth up the length of her arm.

"What? Huh?" He blinked and shook his head. Talk. That's right. He'd come here to talk to her. "Fine. Yeah. Everything's good." Better than fine, really, now that he'd made the toughest decision of his life. "I just left Simon and—"

"Speaking of Simon, his birthday party is going to be fabulous. I got this local band to play—they specialize in big-band music from the forties. I think Simon and his friends will love it."

"I'm sure they will," he said, smiling as she went on about the party. This was the right move to make, he told himself. The two of them were good together. She loved his grandfather. She was already a part of this town.

And while his mind was racing, he thought about Gretchen briefly and wondered why in the hell he'd ever even broached the subject of marriage to her. She would never have fit in here, never have wanted to. Springville was too small, too ordinary, too off-the-beaten-track. Gretchen would have hated this place, while Margie clearly thrived in it.

Yeah. He was doing the right thing.

"And the caterer is going to work with Simon's cook, so everything will be perfect," she said.

"Good."

"Are you okay?" she asked, and the washcloth slowed a bit as she asked the question.

"I am."

He walked into the bathroom, sat down on the edge of the tub and stared down at her. The scent of jasmine was so thick in the air that he drew it into his lungs with every breath, as if she were surrounding him. Her skin was rosy-pink from the hot water, and her lush, dark red curls were wet at the ends. Her lips were full and parted as though she were inviting a kiss, and he was too damn tempted to lean in and give her just what she wanted. But first he had to tell her about the decision he'd made.

Silently, he congratulated himself on finding the perfect solution for all of them and wondered why it had taken so long for him to consider it. Stubborn, like Simon said, he guessed. Didn't matter, though. He saw things clearly now, and he was sure Margie would agree. Why wouldn't she? It was a win-win for both of them.

"Who's Gretchen?" she asked.

"What?" That question threw everything else out of his head.

"I heard you and your friends talking about her when they were here," she said with a shrug that dissipated a few more strategically placed bubbles. "One of them mentioned you and Gretchen."

"Yeah." *Thanks, Hula.* "She's an old girlfriend."

"Ah," she said, dipping the washcloth into the water, then sliding it up her other arm slowly. "And she's a goddess?"

Hunter scowled and watched as the wet cloth slid along her wet skin. Yes, Gretchen was beautiful, but he'd never fantasized about being her washcloth. Besides, he hadn't come up here to talk about Gretchen. "Hula's got a big mouth."

Margie gave him a sad smile. "Which answers my question."

Frowning, he asked, "Why'd you wait until now to ask about her?"

"Maybe because I didn't want to know."

"So why'd you ask at all—" He stopped. "Never mind. This is female logic, right?"

"I was just curious, that's all," she said.

"Fine, but I don't want to talk about my ex or any of your exes, either."

"I don't have any," she told him, sliding her body down into the water until her knees poked through the water's surface and her nipples made tiny pink islands. "Exes, I mean. You'll be my first."

"What?" He stared at her and shook his head, not sure whether to believe that or not. Yes, she'd been a virgin, but she'd had no ex-boyfriends at all? "How is that possible? Do you only meet blind men?"

Margie laughed shortly. "I think that's a compliment, so thanks."

"Of course it's a compliment." Hadn't he complimented her before this? Apparently not. He should have. Hell, she'd stepped up and taken care of Simon when he wasn't around. She'd been there for this town, for his grandfather, for *him*, he thought, remembering the night she'd held him and eased him through a nightmare. The same night they'd had sex for the first time. He'd been so intent on shutting her out, he hadn't told her how much he appreciated everything she did.

But he'd make up for it. He could compliment her plenty over the coming years. He'd make a mental note to do just that. He stood up, not really trusting himself to stay so close to a wet, naked Margie without reaching out a hand to touch, to stroke, to…

"Look, Margie," he said, scraping one hand across his face as if he could wipe away the erotic images filling his mind, "I thought we should talk about the divorce."

"Oh." Her eyes looked suddenly cooler, more distant, as if she were deliberately closing herself off to him. Self-preservation? Probably.

Well, Hunter figured he had the answer to their problems.

"The month's almost up," he said as he walked back to the edge of the tub to look down at her.

"I know."

"Yeah, but you don't know things have changed."

Her gaze lifted to his. "What do you mean?"

"I mean," he said, "that I've decided to leave the Navy when my enlistment's up. I'm coming back home. To stay." Wasn't as hard to say it this time, he thought, and considered that a good sign.

She stilled, then slowly a small smile curved her mouth. "That's wonderful, Hunter. I'm sure Simon's happy."

"Yeah, he is. But I want to talk to you about us."

"I don't understand," she said, using her arms to sweep the remaining bubbles over her, covering her skin in a gleaming, nearly see-through cape.

"I know." He sat down again on the edge of the tub and wished she didn't look so uneasy. "But you will in a minute. I did a little thinking, and I realized there was an easy solution to our situation."

"Yes," she said, huffing out a breath that made the bubbles shudder. "The divorce."

"No," he told her. "The marriage."

She tipped her head up to meet his gaze. "What are you saying?"

"It's simple, really," he said and smiled at her. "I'm staying, so I think you should, too."

"What? Why?" She straightened a little in the water, and the bubbles slid down her skin.

"I'm suggesting that we stay married instead of getting divorced," he told her and waited for her smile.

It didn't come.

"You can't be serious."

"Okay," he admitted, wondering why she wasn't seeing the brilliance of this plan, "not the answer I was expecting."

"Well, you're not making sense," she said, and her voice sounded breathless. "Why would you want to stay married to me? You'll be here, so you won't need me to watch over Simon. You can do it yourself."

"This isn't about Simon," Hunter told her, then corrected himself, "well, it is partly, I suppose. But the main thing is, you love it here, right?"

"Yes..."

"You love Simon."

"Yes, but—"

Hunter was warming to his theme now and gave her a smile designed to convince her to agree. "We've already proven we get along fine. And the sex is good. So why shouldn't we stay married?"

"This is crazy," Margie said softly and stood up in the tub.

Faced with his naked wife, Hunter had a hard time keeping his mind on the subject at hand, but he managed. "What's crazy about it? Hell, I thought you'd be pleased."

She laughed and looked at him as if he were certifiably insane. Stepping out of the tub, she moved past him, grabbed a navy-blue towel off the closest rack and wrapped it around herself. "Oh yeah. Why wouldn't I be pleased?"

"Exactly." He stood up too and glowered at her. Damn it, he'd come up with the perfect solution. Couldn't she see that?

"Hunter," she said, taking a deep breath and holding it, "you've told me over and over that you don't want a wife."

"I changed my mind."

"Oh!" Margie threw both hands up. "Well, that's different, then. You changed your mind."

"What're you pissed about?" He sounded incredulous, as if he didn't understand why she wasn't jumping up and down for joy at his businesslike offer. Couldn't the damn woman see that this was good for both of them? "I thought you'd be happy to stay."

Barefoot, soaking wet and suddenly furious, Margie fisted her hands at her hips. "Why would I be happy to stay with a man who doesn't want me?"

"I just told you I *do* want you."

"Sure, in bed."

"Well, I'm a guy. Why wouldn't I want you in bed?"

"Marriage isn't about sex, Hunter." Shaking her head in disbelief, she turned away from him and started walking. She marched across the bedroom directly into the oversize closet. "My God, don't you get it?"

"Clearly not," he said from right behind her.

She whipped around fast to glare at him. "If I stayed married to you like this, I wouldn't be your wife—I'd be your legal mistress."

"What the hell—"

"You don't love me. I'm just convenient."

Why talk about love now? She'd married him by proxy, and he hadn't even *known* about it. She'd been willing to be *paid* to be his wife. Now she wanted love? What kind of sense did that make?

"Well, yeah, since you are my wife, that makes you pretty damn convenient," he argued. "What's wrong with that?"

"Is it all men?" Margie wondered aloud, shaking her head in exasperation. "Or is it just you?"

"Look, I didn't come up here to fight."

"No, you came to tell me how lucky I was to have been *allowed* to stay in this house and join you in bed." She blew out a breath, fluttered her eyelashes and said, "I'm *such* a lucky woman."

Hunter was lost. First, he was a bastard because he hadn't wanted her. Now, he's the bad guy because he *did?* None of this made sense to him. Why was she making this so hard?

"You know," he said as his features darkened like a thunder cloud, "I—"

"Oh, *and,* I'm even luckier that the great Hunter Cabot is willing to accept plain old Margie Donohue. She's no goddess, but he's willing to put up with his disappointment in that area because she's good with dogs and old people and—"

"Are you insane?" He looked at her as though she were, which only made Margie more furious.

"I should have known this was coming," she muttered to herself as she grabbed the closest pair of jeans and tugged them on. "You're an idiot, Margie. Just an idiot."

"For God's sake, you're taking this all the wrong way," he said tightly.

Inside the closet, Margie fumbled with her bra. "Some fantasy you turned out to be," she mumbled, then shouted, "you are *not* the man I married."

"You *are* crazy!" His shout was louder than hers. "And I never asked to be anyone's fantasy. Just like I never claimed to be a damn hero!" He threw the closet door open and glared at her. "Why bother hiding to dress? Not like I haven't seen you naked often enough."

"And that gives you the right to see me whenever you want to? I don't think so." Margie yanked a dark green T-shirt over her head and yelped when her long, wet hair got caught briefly. "I can't believe you want to keep me around for sex."

Her chest hurt, her eyes stung, but she would *not* cry. For heaven's sake, the first man she'd ever slept with wanted her as a mistress? What did that say about her? His "offer" ran through her mind again. *Stay married. Sex is good.* God, she felt so stupid, so…furious. She'd done this to herself, too. Set herself up for misery. She might as well have walked into his open arms and begged, *Please, Hunter. Break my heart.* And he'd done it.

Worse, he didn't even realize it.

"How could you think I'd agree to that?" she shouted.

"It's not like I asked you to service the fleet," he snarled. "I just thought that we could keep our arrangement going."

"For how long?" she snapped. "Will there be a contract? Severance pay? Oh, will you set up a 401k for me?"

"Margie—"

"And what happens when you 'change your mind' again? Do I get thirty days to find a new place to live, or do I just get tossed out?"

"I'm not going to change my mind again. If you'll just calm down…" His patient tone made her want to kick him.

All of her little dreams and fantasies were popping, just like the bubbles in her bath. They disappeared with hardly a sound, but Margie felt each one go like a crash of thunder. She'd allowed this to happen. She'd built him up in her mind over the last year, and in the last few weeks she'd done even more. She'd fallen in love with a man who didn't exist. The Hunter she wanted, the Hunter she loved would never have made such a suggestion.

So, that let her know exactly what he thought of her. Which only meant that once again, Margie hadn't been good enough.

He stepped up close, cupped her face in his palms and said quietly, "At least think about it, Margie. If you do, you'll see I'm right. You love this place. You love Simon—"

"And I love *you*, Hunter." The minute she said the words, she wanted to call them back. But it was far too late for that.

Instead of dropping his hands and leaping away from her, though, which is totally what she'd expected, Hunter only grinned, and the damn dimple in his cheek taunted her.

"But that makes it even better," he said, sounding like a kid who'd just found exactly what he'd wanted under the Christmas tree. "You love me, so you should want to stay married to me."

She pulled his hands down from her face, and her skin felt cold without his touch. But she'd better get used to that chilly sensation, she told herself, because she could never stay with him now.

"I can't stay with you, Hunter," she said, looking directly into his eyes so he would understand.

"But you love me."

"Which is exactly why I want a divorce."

Ten

The ballroom in the Cabot mansion was beginning to look like a party extravaganza. Decorations were already starting to go up, from banners to colorful ribbons draped along the edges of the ceiling to the linen-draped tables staggered around the room. Tomorrow, there would be multicolored balloons and fresh flowers from the Cabot gardens decorating the tables. The caterers would be in place in the kitchen, and the musicians would be tuning up in the far corner.

Everything was perfect.

So why did Margie feel like crying?

Could it be because of the gaping hole in her chest, where her heart used to be?

Three days since Hunter had made his half-assed proposal and she'd confessed to being in love. Three long days and even longer nights. Right after their little chat, she'd moved her things to a guest room because, frankly, Margie was beyond caring what the household staff thought of the marriage that would soon be ending.

And better she start getting used to sleeping alone than torturing herself by snuggling up beside Hunter every night. But God, she missed him. Missed his touch, his kiss, the way he turned to her in his sleep and wrapped his strong arms around her. How was she supposed to live the rest of her life without him?

Oh, she never should have started this in the first place. If she hadn't agreed to Simon's plan a year ago, she wouldn't be in this fix. By tomorrow night, she'd be leaving. She still didn't know where she'd go. It didn't matter to her, either. Because wherever she ended up, she'd be alone. Again. With no one to love.

"What am I supposed to do now?" she whispered to the empty room.

"Well," a voice said from directly behind her, "you could stop being a damn fool."

"Simon!" Margie whirled around, embarrassed to be caught not only talking to herself but also throwing quite the self-pity party. "I didn't know you were there."

"Not surprising. You've been walking through the house like a ghost these last few days."

What could she say to that? He was absolutely right.

Simon's gaze was kind, but determined. Strange, she'd never noticed just how much he and his grandson had in common.

"Stay, Margie. Stop this foolishness and stay."

"I can't," she said, shaking her head as she looked into Simon's eyes. "I can't stay knowing he doesn't love me."

"Who says he doesn't?"

Margie laughed ruefully. "*He* does."

Simon frowned and brushed that information aside. "He wouldn't be the first man who needed a woman to tell him what he was feeling."

"If only it were that easy."

He shook his head, sending his wispy white hair flying. "You're every bit as stubborn as he is."

"I have to be," she told him. "I can't settle for half a life." Then she gave him a hug. As his arms came around her, she whispered, "I'm really going to miss you."

He patted her back and offered, "I'll beat him up for you if you want."

Margie smiled through her tears. "Thanks, Simon."

As she pulled away, he said, "Still doesn't seem like much of a birthday present for me. You leaving, I mean."

"I wish I could stay. I really do." She let her gaze slide around the room and out to the hall, as if looking all over the mansion she'd come to think of as home. It would be so hard to leave this place. But what choice did she have?

She couldn't stay, loving Hunter and knowing he didn't feel the same. That would be like a slow death. No. Better to go. To move on. Find a new place and try to forget what she'd had so briefly, here.

"It's a shame you don't love him enough to fight for him," Simon mused.

Surprised, Margie only said, "I do love him enough. But Simon, you can't fight a battle you can't win."

"Ah," he said solemnly, "sometimes those are the only battles worth fighting."

An hour later, there was a knock at the door, and when Margie opened it, a tall, elegantly dressed, absolutely breathtaking woman swept inside.

"Isn't this lovely." The blonde's cool blue eyes swept the interior of the mansion as if she were taking an inventory. Then she glanced at Margie, giving her a quick, dismissive glance as if finding her less than interesting.

Margie's spine stiffened a little in response. For the moment, this was her house and this blonde was the intruder, gorgeous though she might be.

"Can I help you?"

"Yes." The blonde looked down from her towering height and gave a smile that barely creased her lean cheeks. "You can tell Hunter that Gretchen is here to see him."

"Gretchen?" Margie could have sworn she felt a cold, hard piece of ice settle in the pit of her stomach. *This* was Hunter's ex-girlfriend? Oh dear God. No wonder his friend Hula had called her a goddess and had been so surprised to find out that Margie was Hunter's wife. In comparison with this—okay, *goddess* really was the only appropriately descriptive word—Margie felt like Cinderella. *Before* the big night with her fairy godmother.

"Yes. Is Hunter here?" The blonde walked farther down the hall, peeked into the living room, then turned back. "I was going to call him, but then I thought what fun it would be to surprise him."

"You have," Hunter said from the staircase.

Margie looked over her shoulder at him and tried to read his expression. His features were tight, his eyes shuttered and his jawline grim. Well, at least he didn't look delighted to see the fabulous Gretchen.

"Hunter, honey!" The tall blond actually squealed as she raced to his side on incredibly long legs.

Margie stood open-mouthed and watched as Gretchen flung herself at Hunter's chest. He caught her automatically, and for one brief moment the two of them were locked together. Margie's stomach lurched again. *This* was the kind of woman Hunter belonged with, she told herself. No wonder he wasn't interested in a ten-pound-overweight, curly-haired redhead with freckles in all the wrong places.

Hunter's gaze locked with hers over Gretchen's shoulder, and he looked frustrated. He tried to mouth something at her, but then the blonde pulled back, looked up at him and said, "I came to tell you I've decided I *will* marry you, after all!"

Margie's jaw dropped and her eyes narrowed as the rest of her world dissolved out from under her.

"Damn it." Hunter saw the look in Margie's eyes as he pried Gretchen's long fingers off his shoulders and set her onto her feet. His ex was babbling, but he wasn't listening. Instead, he was focused on the short redhead glaring at him. There was fury and pain mingling in Margie's green eyes, and Hunter wished Gretchen to the other side of the planet.

"Margie, I can explain," he said, and did some mental sprints trying to figure out just *what* he could say. And in the next instant, he reminded himself that she hadn't listened to him for the last few days, so why would she start now?

"Oh, there's nothing *to* explain, Hunter," she said from her position by the front door. "Really. Everything's very clear."

"Hunter, who is this person?" Gretchen's voice had a spike in it as if she were less than amused.

"Don't you worry about me," Margie told her with a way-too-sweet smile. "I'm just his wife."

"His *wife?*" she cried, with a gaping look at Margie. "Seriously?"

Hunter almost clapped one hand over Gretchen's mouth, but it wouldn't have helped anyway. Instead, he glared at her. "How the hell did you find me?"

"Well, you told me the name of your little town. Wasn't hard to find the only Cabots here."

"Right." So this was his own damn fault. He looked past the blonde. "Margie—"

"Hunter," Margie said as the toe of her tennis shoe tapped noisily against the floor, "don't you want to invite your fiancée in for a drink?"

"No," he shouted and tried to get past Gretchen, but the blonde latched onto his upper arm with strong fingers and deadly nails. "And she's not my fiancée."

"Yes, I am," Gretchen argued. "That's what I came here to tell you. And then I find you're already married."

"I never asked you to marry me," Hunter countered with a triumphant look at Margie.

"You said you were thinking about getting married

and asked me what I thought about the idea," she reminded him.

"How very romantic," Margie mused.

"It was an abstract idea," Hunter shouted.

"Is there a problem?" the housekeeper asked as she came running down the long hallway.

"Yes, Sophie," Margie told her, "would you bring Hunter and his fiancée some tea in the front parlor?"

"His what?" Sophie's big eyes slitted and focused on the tall blonde.

"She's not my fiancée," Hunter argued.

"Yes, I am," Gretchen said.

"Oh, how nice. Must be true love," Margie said and clasped both hands under her chin. "Isn't that special?"

"Damn it, Margie, you know this is all a mistake."

"Mistake?" Gretchen echoed, giving him a glare that could have fried bacon.

"Yes, a mistake. I can't be engaged, I'm already married," Hunter said and felt like he was talking to an empty room. Not one of the three women glaring at him was listening to him. They were all talking to one another and around him, but it was as if he weren't there.

"Not for long," Margie told him flatly.

"There," Gretchen said, looking very pleased, "problem solved."

When he gave Gretchen an impatient look, she blinked at him and worked up a pout. He'd seen her do it before and knew she could manage to squeeze out a theatrical tear or two if she had to, just as easily. And he really didn't have time for Gretchen's drama.

"Hunter, make that woman go away so we can talk."

"She's not going anywhere, and we have nothing to talk about," he ground out.

"But surely you want to make some wedding plans," Margie taunted and folded her arms across her chest. "After all, the divorce will be final soon—no sense wasting time."

"Divorce?" Gretchen smiled again.

"There's not going to be a divorce," Hunter said.

"Don't count on it," Margie muttered, then turned to Sophie. "Would you mind helping me out in the ballroom? I want to do another check on the party things."

"Yes, ma'am," Sophie said and gave Hunter a hard glare he hadn't seen since he was thirteen years old.

Could this day go to hell any faster?

"Margie, wait." Damn it. She'd hardly spoken to him in the last few days, and now with Gretchen showing up out of the blue things just got even more difficult. But Margie left, without so much as a glance over her shoulder, and he was faced with a tall blonde from his past giving him a cool, calculating stare.

"Just what is going on here, Hunter?" Gretchen smoothed her hair unnecessarily, then tapped the tip of her index finger against her chin. "I don't appreciate being made to look like a fool."

"I didn't invite you here, Gretchen," he reminded her, flicking a glance down the hall where Margie had gone.

She ignored that remark. "Strange that you never mentioned the fact that you were already married when we were together."

"It's a long story." And he wouldn't come out sounding too good in it, either. After all, he had been legally married while he was dating Gretchen. The fact that he hadn't known about the marriage would really be a hard sell.

But he knew it for a fact, so why did he feel like a cheating husband caught sneaking out of a motel?

"I'm sure," Gretchen said tightly. "Oddly enough, I'm not interested enough to hear it. I don't date married men, Hunter."

"Good for you," he said, easing her down the stairs with a tight grip on her elbow. "Then you should be going, right?"

He just wanted her the hell out of the house so he could talk to Margie. Make her understand. Make her see that he didn't want Gretchen. He wanted *her.*

Gretchen wouldn't be hurried, though. She glanced around the great hall, noting the stained glass, the polished wood and the obvious signs of a great deal of money. "But if you're in the process of a divorce, that changes things considerably. You know I'm happy to wait for you."

"No," he snapped, meeting her gaze with a hard look. "Don't bother waiting, Gretchen. I told you, there's not going to be a divorce." At least, not if he could find a way around it.

"Well then, it seems I've made a mistake," she said, her voice dropping to a low purr as she dragged the tips of her fingers down his chest. "Unless, of course, I can change your mind…."

Though Gretchen was planning a seduction, all Hunter felt was irritation. "You should go, Gretchen. Sorry you wasted the trip."

Instantly, she straightened up, dropped the sultry, heavy-lidded gaze and snapped, "Fine. Go to your fat little redhead. May you be cursed with a dozen fat babies who look just like her."

Babies? Instantly, an image of Margie carrying his child filled his mind, and Hunter realized he *wanted* that reality. He wanted Margie in his life more completely than he'd ever wanted anything. And he wanted kids. With her. Damned if he'd let her walk away from what they could have together.

Gretchen, meanwhile, huffed out a breath and swept out of the house as majestically as only a six-foot-tall, skinny model with delusions of grandeur could muster. Hunter shut the door behind her and took a long, deep breath. She never had taken rejection well.

How in the hell could he even briefly have considered a life with her? The drama. The pouting. The grasping nature. The viciousness. Margie wasn't fat. She was curvy, deliciously curvy. And kind. And good-hearted. And she loved him.

So why the hell didn't she want to stay married to him?

Eleven

The party was everything Margie had hoped it would be. As her big farewell to the town of Springville and Simon, it was perfect. The fact that the smile she'd plastered on her face was almost painful to maintain was no one else's business.

Dance music soared through the air, and candles in glass bowls flickered on every table. Clusters of spring flowers made for bright splashes of color, and their scents mingled with the delicious aromas coming from the kitchen as the catering crew ran up and down the long hallway to the ballroom.

Balloons festooned every corner of the massive room, and there was a cheerful fire in the hearth at the far end of the room to combat the cool, nighttime breeze drifting in through the open French doors. The floors gleamed under the light thrown from the chandeliers, and in the backyard, fairy lights were strung in the trees ringing the garden. Everything was fabulous, and Simon's guests were all clearly having a good time.

"Yay me," Margie whispered as she rubbed her hands up and down her arms against the tiny chill snaking along her skin. But it didn't help, because this cold went bone-deep. This was the cold she was far too familiar with.

The cold of alone. The cold of unwanted. Unchosen. Not really even a word, she told herself, but it was so true. No one in her whole damn life had ever chosen her. She'd never been first. She'd never been important enough to matter.

And God, she'd so wanted to matter to Hunter.

Against her will, her gaze scanned the crowd for one man in particular. He wasn't hard to find. Wearing his dress whites uniform, Hunter Cabot looked impossibly handsome. Simply watching him made her heartbeat quicken and curls of heat spiral in the pit of her stomach. He was standing with his grandfather in a circle of friends, and Margie felt like the outsider she'd always been.

She had no place here. Not anymore. She shouldn't have even stayed for the party, but she'd felt that she owed it to Simon. Now, she wished she were anywhere but here.

"This is great, Margie," someone said from nearby, and she turned to foist her phony smile on Terry Gates. Terry was yet another friend she'd made here in Springville. Another person she'd miss. Another link lost in her own personal chain.

"Thanks, Terry," she managed to say past the hard lump in her throat. "I'm so glad you could come."

"Are you kidding? Wouldn't have missed it." Terry's green eyes danced as she leaned in. "The whole town's here."

"Seems like," she mused, her gaze once again going unerringly toward the man who was and *wasn't* her husband.

"Hmm..." Terry gave her a little nudge. "Why are you standing here alone when you should be dancing with that gorgeous man of yours?"

Because to dance with him to this music would mean being in Hunter's arms, and how could Margie ever force herself to leave that warm circle once she'd willingly gone into it? Better to keep her distance. Better to save whatever pride she had left and remember what Hunter had looked like with Gretchen. They'd actually made a gorgeous couple.

Blast it.

But Terry was watching her, waiting for an answer. "Oh, too busy to dance. Have to keep track of the caterers and—"

"Not a chance," Terry said with a laugh and grabbed hold of Margie's elbow. "You arranged it all, did all the work, and now you're going to take a minute to dance with your husband."

"No, really, I um—" Margie tried to pull away, but she couldn't get any traction out of the needle-thin high heels she was wearing with the strapless black dress Hunter had picked out for her what seemed like a lifetime ago. "I really need to—"

"Dance," Terry told her firmly and kept walking, threading their way through the crowd.

"Oh, for—" Margie stopped trying to argue, stopped

trying to fight her way free of her friend's good intentions. The more she struggled, the more attention she garnered from the watching crowd, and she was determined that no one here would know that her heart was breaking—or that her marriage was over as of tonight.

"Atta girl," Terry said, sensing the difference in her friend's attitude. Then she smiled and shrugged. "Look, I shouldn't say anything, but I know."

"Know?" Margie asked as they slowed down to get through a knot of people.

"About your argument with Hunter," Terry said with a shrug.

Oh, God. How could she know? Who would have said anything? Not Simon or Sophie. Surely not Hunter.

"He told me," Terry was saying. "Hunter said you were mad at him because he was going back to base before he was completely healed."

"Oh." Confused, Margie shifted her gaze from Terry to Hunter, who was watching their approach with a half smile on his face. "He told you that, did he?"

"Yeah, and between us, I so agree. But I feel bad for him that you're not speaking to him, so that's why I agreed to go and get you to dance with him."

"*Hunter* put you up to this?"

"Who else, silly?"

Who else indeed, Margie thought as she came to a stop right in front of the very man she'd been ignoring for days. The very man who held every corner of her heart. The man she'd never forget and would miss every day of her life.

His blue eyes locked with her green ones and he gave her a small, intimate smile that just barely nudged his dimple into existence. Without looking at the other woman, he said quietly, "Thanks, Terry."

"No problem," the brunette said, then turned her head to look out over the crowd. "Now, think I'll go find my own husband and force him to dance with me."

Hunter stepped up close to Margie and her heart did a quick, hard *thump*. His eyes were so deep, so clear and so intent on her that she couldn't have looked away if her life had depended on it.

"Dance with me, Margie," he said and held out one hand to her.

The people around them were watching—she could feel it. To one side of Hunter, Simon stood looking like a benevolent elf with his flyaway white hair and smiling blue eyes. Could she really turn away? Did she want to make everyone talk about them, wonder what was wrong between them? Wouldn't it be easier if no one knew a thing until she'd gone?

Besides all that, could she really pass up the chance to be held by him one last time?

Finally nodding, Margie slipped her hand into Hunter's, and instant warmth slid through her bloodstream, temporarily easing the cold inside her. He led her onto the dance floor just as the band ended one song and started another.

Margie recognized the tune, since Simon was a huge Frank Sinatra fan. And though the band's singer was no Ol' Blue Eyes, the melody and words of the song about a summer wind wrapped themselves around her and Hunter and drew them into the magic of the moment.

"You look beautiful tonight," he said, his voice a low rush of sensuality that seemed to slide right inside Margie.

"Thanks." She looked up into his eyes, felt her heart break a little and then shifted her gaze to one side. She couldn't look into his blue eyes. Couldn't read the regrets and goodbyes written there.

"You've been avoiding me," he said and moved her into a slow turn that made the lights at the edges of her vision swim.

"Yes." God, would this dance never end? Margie tried to pull back from Hunter's embrace, to put a little space between them, but he wouldn't allow that. Instead, he pulled her closer, held her more tightly, pressed her body into the length of his until she felt his heartbeat pounding in tandem with her own.

"I don't want you to go, Margie. Don't leave."

"Don't do this," she whispered brokenly. "Don't make it harder."

"It should be hard. You said you loved me."

She looked up at him, and it seemed as though every light in the room was reflected in his gaze. Those blue depths sparkled and shone down at her, and it took all of her courage to not look away. "I do," she said, forcing the words out. "I do love you, and that's why I won't stay."

His arm tightened around her even further until it felt as though she could hardly draw a breath. "I wasn't engaged to Gretchen."

Margie closed her eyes briefly, gathered up her strength and made herself ask, "Did you propose to her?"

The music pumped around them, other dancers drifted past and Hunter looked only at her. "In a way I guess I did," he said. "But—"

"No. You *wanted* Gretchen," she said as the song

slowly wound its way to the end. "You never wanted me. I wasn't your choice for a wife. She was."

"But she's not my wife. You are."

She shook her head. "It doesn't matter, Hunter. Don't you get it? It just doesn't matter."

The music ended, but Hunter wouldn't let her go. He stood there, on the dance floor, his arms still holding her tight, his gaze locked with hers, refusing to say goodbye. To let her walk away. From him.

"Of course it matters," he said, his voice low and dark, filled with a banked anger that nibbled at the edges of his self-control. Hell, he'd given her days to get past this hang-up of hers. Days to think about his offer. To reconsider. To stay the hell married to him. And this is what it was going to come down to? A quick goodbye on a dance floor, surrounded by too many damn people?

He didn't think so.

As if she could read his mind, she whispered, "Please don't do this, Hunter. Don't make it harder."

"It damn well *should* be hard," he told her, his voice low and hot with a temper crouched inside him.

She was bound and determined to walk away from him, and Hunter simply wasn't going to let that happen. Never once in his SEAL career had he given up on reaching his objective. He'd had guns misfire, plans go askew, ambushes fail, but he'd *always* won the day. Damned if he was going to ruin his record now.

His chest felt tight and his insides snapped to attention. Releasing her briefly, he then took her upper arm in a firm grip and turned her toward the French doors and the gardens beyond.

"Okay, that's it. You're coming with me."

"Oh no, I'm not," Margie countered and pulled free of his hold. Then she took two long steps in the opposite direction, obviously headed for the foyer.

"Like hell," Hunter muttered and caught up to her in a flat second. Spinning her around to face him, he held on to her shoulders, met her now furious, embarrassed gaze and said, "You're going to listen to me, Margie, even if I have to tie you to a chair."

From somewhere to his right, he absentmindedly heard his grandfather's chuckle. Well, Hunter was glad somebody was enjoying this.

"*Hunter...*" Her gaze shot from side to side, then up to him, as if to point out to him that they weren't exactly alone.

Hunter couldn't have cared less. Glaring at her, he said, "You think I give a good damn who's watching?"

"Well, I do."

"I don't. I've got some things to say to you, and I'm going to say 'em. Here or somewhere else. Your choice."

Margie glanced around again and apparently noticed the eager attention on the faces surrounding them. She finally looked up at him and said, "Fine. We can talk in the study."

"Nope, too far away," he told her and bent down. Tucking his shoulder into her abdomen, he straightened up with her head and shoulders now hanging down over his back.

"*What are you doing?*" she shrieked it, pushing herself up from his back and trying to shove herself free.

"What I should have done three days ago," Hunter

told her and threw one arm across her legs, pinning her to him.

"Simon!" Margie yelled as Hunter headed for the French doors, "help me!"

"Not a chance, honey," the old man shouted on a laugh.

The whole room was laughing, Hunter realized as the crowd parted before him and let him pass through the ballroom and into the gardens. And he didn't care. Didn't care what they thought, what they had to say or the fact that they'd be talking about this night for the next twenty years.

Nothing mattered but the stubborn redhead in his arms. And no way was he going to lose her.

Jaw tight, body rigid, he marched across the patio, muttering, "Excuse me," to those he passed.

"Let me down!" Margie shouted, then in a much lower voice adding, "You're showing the whole world my behind, you know!"

Hunter grinned, gave that sweet rear end of hers a friendly smack and told her, "It's a great behind. You've got nothing to be ashamed of."

"For heaven's sake, Hunter, put me down!"

"Soon." He kept walking. Hell, he knew these paths better than Calvin. This was home, and he felt as though the fairy lights in the trees and the garden itself were welcoming him back.

"Where are we going?" she demanded.

"To the fountain." It was the most secluded spot on the grounds. Surrounded by trees and flowering bushes, the old fountain was so far back, so near the edge of the cliff overlooking the ocean that almost no one went out there anymore. Much of the cliff's edge had been eroded over the years, so it wasn't the safest place on the estate. Therefore, Hunter told himself, none of the guests would be wandering out there.

He and Margie could be alone, and for what he wanted to say, he needed them to be alone.

When he set her onto her feet, she staggered a little, tossed her hair back out of her face and took a wild swing at him. He caught her fist in one hand, then bent and kissed her knuckles.

"Don't do that." She pulled her hand free and looked around wildly.

Hunter did too, just to check the area. There was no one there, and the only sound besides the wind in the trees was the soft hush of the ocean below and the cheerful splash of the fountain.

"Margie, Gretchen doesn't mean a thing to me," he started.

She blew out a breath, shook her head and said, "If you think that makes me feel better, you're wrong."

"I'm not finished," he snapped, watching as moonlight shimmered in her eyes. "There's something I need to say to you, and you're going to listen."

"There's nothing you can say, Hunter." Her voice broke, and something inside him twisted in response. She looked so lost, so lovely there in the moonlight. The ocean breeze twisted itself in her curls, and her eyes were wide, glimmering with the reflection of the moonlight. "Nothing's going to change my mind. I'm leaving."

He looked at her fiercely brave expression and felt an explosion of knowledge open up inside him. Couldn't figure out why he hadn't seen it before, because right now the truth was so crystal clear it was as if he'd been born knowing it. He didn't just want her. Didn't just need her. It was so much more than that.

"I love you," he said and smiled at the wonder of saying those words and meaning them with everything he had.

She gasped and looked up at him. Then she shook her head. "No, no, you don't. You only want me to stay because I'm already your wife. I'm easy."

Hunter laughed shortly, loudly. "Margie, you are many things, but you haven't been *easy* since the day we met."

She frowned at him.

"And I love you."

"Stop saying that."

"No," he told her, coming closer. "I like saying it. I like *feeling* it."

"No," she argued, her voice hardly more than a murmur, "you don't."

"Yeah, I do. And I'm going to say it until you believe me. I'll say it every damn day for the rest of our lives and find a way to say it after I'm dead, if that's what it takes to convince you."

"Hunter…" She bit down on her bottom lip, brushed a single tear from her cheek and turned away from him to stare out at the ocean and the moonlight striping its surface like a pathway to heaven.

"Why is that so hard to believe?"

She huffed out a breath, wrapped her arms around herself and whispered, "Because no one's ever loved me."

Her pain whipped through him with a hell of a lot

more force than that bullet had. He felt her broken heart and wanted to kick his own ass for ever bringing her to tears. "What do you mean?"

She shook her head, and her hair moved with the wind sighing past them. "I didn't grow up like you did, Hunter. I grew up in a series of foster homes that were never really mine."

Moving softly, quietly, Hunter laid his hands on her shoulders and stroked his palms down her arms. "I'm sorry for that, Margie. I am. But you have to believe, I do love you."

She sniffed, breathed fast and shook her head. "You have to stop saying it, Hunter. Please. Stop."

He turned her in his arms, never taking his hands from her, needing to feel her, needing her to feel his touch. To somehow understand just what she was to him.

"Margie, why can't you believe me? Why can't you see that I want you to be with me? Forever."

Crying now, in big gulping sobs, she turned her gaze up to his and said, "Because no one ever has. Never once, Hunter. In my whole life I've never been chosen. I've never been important to somebody. Until I came here. And Simon loved me. And I loved this place and convinced myself that I loved *you.*"

He took a harsh breath and held it, wanting to hear her out, wanting her to get it all said so they could start again. Start fresh.

"But Hunter, you didn't *choose* me to be your wife." She sniffed again and waved one hand at the mansion behind them. "You picked a Swedish goddess. You didn't want me. You just got stuck with *me.* And now you're trying to do the right thing. But you're only making it harder—can't you see that?"

Shaken to his soul, Hunter wondered how he'd ever gotten lucky enough to have this woman tossed into his life. What had he done that had merited this warm, loving, gentle heart? And how could he keep her?

"You're wrong," he said and smiled in spite of the fresh bout of tears his words started. "I'm choosing you now, Margie. I know you. I love you. And I'm choosing you."

She still didn't believe him, and her tears were falling fast and furiously. Cupping her face in his palms, Hunter tipped her face up to his. Then he bent, kissed her cheeks and tasted the salt of her tears.

"Listen to me, *babe,*" he said, using that word deliberately to make her roll her eyes and smile.

It worked, though that fragile curve of her lips was tremulous.

"You said no one ever wanted you to stay, Margie. Well, I do. I *need* you to stay here with me."

"Oh, God..." She shook her head as if she were tempted to believe but still too afraid of losing everything to take the chance.

Hunter looked deeply into her eyes, willing her to see all that he was feeling. "Margie, I've been in combat. I've been in situations so dark and terrifying I never thought I'd survive. I've faced gunfire, bombs and explosions with more ease than I can face the thought of living a life without you."

She blew out a breath that ruffled the curls on her forehead. Then her mouth worked as she tried to stem the tears that continued to rain down her face. "Hunter..."

"I've got seven more months in the Navy, Margie. Then I'm coming home. To a place that *you* made me see I belonged. I'm coming home to you, Margie. And if you're not here, it won't be *home.*"

"Hunter, you're not being fair," she murmured, shaking her head again and taking a shuddering breath. "I was going to leave and let you have your life back."

He laughed because he finally sensed that he was convincing her, and, God, he felt better than he had in years.

"My life? What kind of life would it be without you ordering me around? Without you organizing everything? Without you to hold in the night? Without you to wake up to? If you leave me, Margie," he added, and waited until she was looking into his eyes, so she could read just how serious he really was. "If you leave me, I'll follow you. I'll turn into some weirdo stalker, and then Simon'll be alone and the town will fall apart because you're not here to be the heart of it…." He paused and smiled gently. "Do you really want to be responsible for all of that?"

She sniffed again and smiled a little. "Well, if you put it like that…"

He gathered her in close, folding his arms around her, resting his chin on top of her head, and when she wrapped her arms around his middle, Hunter took his first easy breath in days. "You're right where you belong, Margie. With me."

"Oh, God," she said, leaning back and brushing at the front of his uniform, "I'm getting mascara all over your whites!"

Hunter laughed, delighted. "You can cry on me anytime you want to," he said, "but I swear, I'll try to make sure none of your tears are because of me."

"I do love you," she said.

"I love you, Margie." Then to make sure she heard his next words, he held her face in his hands again and looked directly into her eyes. "*You* are the most important thing in my life. I choose *you* to love forever. I choose *you* to make me complete and to make a family with. Please choose me back."

"Oh God, I'm gonna cry again," she said with a half laugh.

"Well, then, let's make sure it's worth it," he said, giving her a fast, hard kiss. "Here's something else for you to organize."

"What?"

"When I come home, you and I are going to have a real wedding. Right here in town," he told her, bending down to lift her into the curve of his arms.

"We are?" Margie grinned up at him and wrapped her arms around his neck.

"We damn sure are," he told her with a wink. "And *then,* we're going to Bali. I think we can improve on that 'honeymoon' we already had, don't you?"

"I don't know," Margie teased, "in my fantasies, you were pretty good…"

"Babe," he said, grinning down at her with a wink, "I'm a SEAL. I love a challenge."

Laughing, her heart lighter than it had ever been, Margie laid her cheek against her own personal hero's shoulder and let him carry her back into the light.

Back to the house where love waited.

* * * * *

"I'VE FOUND HER."

Max froze.

It was what he'd been waiting for since June, but now—now he was almost afraid to voice the question. His heart stalling, he leaned slowly back in his chair and scoured the investigator's face for clues. "Where?" he asked, and his voice sounded rough and unused, like a rusty hinge.

"In Suffolk. She's living in a cottage."

Living. His heart crashed back to life, and he sucked in a long, slow breath. All these months he'd feared—

"Is she well?"

"Yes, she's well."

He had to force himself to ask the next question. "Alone?"

The man paused. "No. The cottage belongs to a man called John Blake. He's working away at the moment, but he comes and goes."

God. He felt sick. So sick he hardly registered the next few words, but then gradually they sank in. "She's got *what?*"

"Babies. Twin girls. They're eight months old."

"Eight—?" he echoed under his breath. "They must be his."

He was thinking out loud, but the P.I. heard and corrected him.

"Apparently not. I gather they're hers. She's been there since mid-January last year, and they were born during the summer—June, the woman in the post office thought. She was more than helpful. I think there's been a certain amount of speculation about their relationship."

He'd just bet there had. God, he was going to kill her. Or Blake. Maybe both of them.

"Of course, looking at the dates, she was presumably pregnant when she left you, so they could be yours, or she could have been having an affair with this Blake character before…"

He glared at the unfortunate P.I. "Just stick to your job. I can do the math," he snapped, swallowing the unpalatable possibility that she'd been unfaithful to him before she'd left. "Where is she? I want the address."

"It's all in here," the man said, sliding a large envelope across the desk to him. "With my invoice."

"I'll get it seen to. Thank you."

"If there's anything else you need, Mr. Gallagher, any further information—"

"I'll be in touch."

"The woman in the post office told me Blake was away at the moment, if that helps," he added quietly, and opened the door.

Max stared down at the envelope, hardly daring to open it, but when the door clicked softly shut behind the P.I., he eased up the flap, tipped it and felt his breath jam in his throat as the photos spilled out over the desk.

Oh, lord, she looked gorgeous. Different, though. It took him a moment to recognize her, because she'd grown her hair, and it was tied back in a ponytail, making her look younger and somehow freer. The blond highlights were gone, and it was back to its natural soft golden-brown, with a little curl in the end of the ponytail that he wanted to thread his finger through and tug, just gently, to draw her back to him.

Crazy. She'd put on a little weight, but it suited her. She looked well and happy and beautiful, but oddly, considering how desperate he'd been for news of her for the past year—one year, three weeks and two days, to be exact—it wasn't only Julia who held his attention after the initial shock. It was the babies sitting side by side in a supermarket trolley. Two identical and absolutely beautiful little girls.

* * * * *

COMING NEXT MONTH

#1921 MR. STRICTLY BUSINESS—Day Leclaire
Man of the Month
He'd always taken what he wanted, when he wanted it—but she wouldn't bend to those rules. Now she needs his help. His price? Her—back in his bed.

#1922 TEMPTED INTO THE TYCOON'S TRAP—Emily McKay
The Hudsons of Beverly Hills
When he finds out that her secret baby is really his, he demands that she marry him. But their passion hasn't fizzled, and soon their marriage of convenience becomes very real.

#1923 CONVENIENT MARRIAGE, INCONVENIENT HUSBAND—Yvonne Lindsay
Rogue Diamonds
She'd left him at the altar eight years ago, but now she needs him in order to gain her inheritance. Could this be his chance to teach her that one can't measure love with money?

#1924 RESERVED FOR THE TYCOON—Charlene Sands
Suite Secrets
His new events planner is trying to sabotage his hotel, but his attraction to her is like nothing he's ever felt. Will he choose to destroy her...or seduce her?

#1925 MILLIONAIRE'S SECRET SEDUCTION—Jennifer Lewis
The Hardcastle Progeny
On discovering a beautiful woman's intentions to sue his father's company, he makes her a deal—her body in exchange for his silence.

#1926 THE C.O.O. MUST MARRY—Maxine Sullivan
Their fathers forced them to marry each other to save their families' fortunes. Will a former young love blossom again, or will secrets drive them apart?

SDCNMBPA0109